My Little Brother Ray
and
Rose - a Wonderful I

Hope you'll take the time
to read this.

Love
Doreen
Dec 2009

Easton Lee

Second published in Jamaica, 2008 by
BalaPress
10 Hopedale Avenue
Kingston 6
Jamaica, W. I.

ISBN 978 976 8217 10 3

Cover painting by Kevin Bergeron

Book design by Kreswick Designs

Printed by World Printing Inc., Miami FL

National Library of Jamaica Cataloguing-in-Publication Data

Lee, Easton
    Run big 'fraid- and other village stories / Easton Lee

    p. ; cm.

ISBN 978 976 8217 10 3 (pbk)

1 Jamaican fiction   2. Short stories, Jamaica

1 Title

813   dc 22

Dedication

To the ancestral spirits
To my Jamaican grandfather -Hubert Paul Simpson
To Aunt Jane Lindon
To Uncle Joe Holness
To all the other old people all over rural Jamaica - "*humble and not so humble country folk*"

To my father and the Chinese relatives - all whose life I have shared and from whom I have learnt so much, whose wisdom and teaching I value and treasure

All of us who have benefited from that lore and learning, have an obligation to pass on this heritage to those who come after us.

Easton

Acknowledgements

My very special thanks and deep appreciation to:
My dear wife Jean, who is supportive of all my efforts; my nieces Sandy Oquendo and Donnette Chin-Loy whose regard I treasure; Ruth Ho-Shing for the typing of the manuscript; Kevin Bergeron for cover painting; Kreswick Designs for book design and layout; Lisa Morgan for proofing the manuscript; my dear friend Glynis Salmon, who served as Managing Editor and Publishing Manager; and to BalaPress the Publishing House whose vision I share and support even as it serves to support my publication.

Thanks to you: family, friends and community, who may have shared a tale or two with me; or may have encouraged me through my literary journey; or stand ready to include the finished product in your Caribbean Stories collection. Whatever your contribution may have been, thank you for your energy and positive vibrations, which has moved this book from a mere idea to printed reality.

May you all enjoy the fruit of all your labours, interest, support and your goodwill. Bless you all.

Thanks be to God.

Easton

Preface

This collection of short stories, like my first two books of poems, are tales and lore from my childhood. They are all true, none is invented but names have been changed for obvious reasons. This time they are mostly in prose and the reported speech in the vernacular.

Growing up in a grocery shop in a rural Jamaican village you could not escape hearing the stories, the gossip and the news you did. You heard "the good, the bad and the indifferent".

Day after day, everyday, every hour of the day there was someone at the counter relating the happenings, sometimes in the most graphic and explicit detail, about everybody and anybody. Much private and confidential information was spoken as these tales were exchanged. One of the most amusing and usual prefaces to a piece of gossip was, "No say a me say, but meck mi tell yu how it go".

So these stories are about real people as they lived their lives in a remote Jamaican setting. Some are sad and may perhaps evoke a tear, others amusing making you laugh, one or two a little risqué, still others might make you think. Many have much to teach us about ourselves and our people in those times of our grand and great grandparents, how they survived at a time when there were none of the modern amenities and conveniences we now take for granted. You may learn something of our ancestral lore and ancient wisdom, much of which we have lost or discarded or forgotten in our embracing of alien cultures. These are certainly glimpses of what life was like for our people not so long ago.

It is my hope that you enjoy reading these stories as much as I enjoyed recalling them.

Easton Lee

Contents

Argument

Aunt Elle and Maas Josiah were second cousins, "born and grow" in the same district, went to the same school, the same church, bathed in the same river, had the same friends and relatives. There was only one thing that wasn't the same, the difference in their ages. Aunt Elle was about four years older than Maas Josiah. But according to what the old people say, he was a fast grower; by the time he was twelve he was a big boy for his age, she was a petite young miss, a little small for her age. They grew up together like good cousins should for they had the example of their parents and grandparents to follow.

They lived good with each other until Elle at age twenty-one married a young farmer from Westmoreland and went to live in that parish. Poor Josiah was heartbroken. For years, ever since he could remember, he had had special likeness for Elle, but he had kept his feelings much to himself and not many people knew of it. So when his father returned from a trip to his uncle in St. Thomas and indicated that the coconut farm that his uncle had inherited from his father-in-law was going well and that he was asking Josiah to come and work with him as a partner, Josiah jumped at the idea.

"Is a good decision you making," his father told him, "you gran uncle is not as young as he used to be and you know he don't have anyone to assist him – one day that property could be yours if you play your cards right."

Maas Josiah agreed and the same year, in fact the next month after Elle got married and went to Westmoreland to live, he went to the opposite end of the island to St. Thomas to work with his grand-uncle.

That was nearly seventy years ago. During that time, Miss Elle had six children and fifteen grandchildren and eight greatgrands. She buried her first husband and married again to a wealthy man from neighbouring St. James and lived a happy prosperous life. After her second husband died, she went to the United States of America and spent a few years with her eldest daughter by the first husband who was a doctor in a big children's hospital over there and was doing very well.

Miss Conse was telling what was one of her favourite stories. Matter of fact, all her children were holding good jobs, both at home and abroad. And her grandchildren too were all up and coming professional people. One grandson had his own large prosperous business.

There was no question about it, Miss Elle was living a good life, adored by all her children and their children to the third generation, a loving and caring family. She had health and strength and in her ninetieth year was considered a blessed soul. In all this she had not lost her sense of humour and the qualities that made her a jolly old lady. Looking at her you couldn't really tell that she was that old. She looked like a spry woman in her seventies, and young seventies at that.

Strangely enough, in all these years she had not returned to the district, except when her mother died many, many years ago and she took her father to live with her in St. James.

Maas Josiah had married and settled down after his many letters to Miss Elle went unanswered. He too had raised a prosperous family. He had eight children in all, five sons and three daughters, and he also had a number of grandchildren and great-grandchildren, all doing well, making him proud and his life happy and prosperous. He, unlike Miss Elle, made frequent trips back to the district for one reason or another. On every occasion he did not fail to ask other relatives for news about Miss Elle. For all these years they had not seen each other. But he made sure to find out all he could. The interest he displayed each time no doubt aroused the curiosity of those from whom he sought information. But nobody paid serious attention to that, except to remark, "after all it look as if Maas Josiah still like off Miss Elle."

Only, of course, Miss Constance pursued the matter as she did all the stories going around. "You know Miss Vie, from me was a little girl me hear my great-aunt talking about that same affair between Maas Josiah and Miss Elle."

Miss Constance was putting the last of the buttons on the shirt she had just finished for her nephew. "But Miss Conse, according to how the story really go, there is nothing between them, Maas Josiah like her but she not interested," Miss Vie said, helping her to fold the shirt.

"Well mam, if it was me, me wouldn't interested either, for Josiah too wild."

And Miss Vie thought, "better a wild one than none at all, that's why you end up on the shelf like dead stock inna Uncle Young shop." But Miss Vie didn't say anything as she didn't want to start any argument with Miss Conse. That would be a whole day affair and she just didn't have the time today.

Well, when the news broke that there was going to be a big gathering of the Williams clan for the wedding of Maas Charley's first daughter, excitement ran high. Miss Conse explained that, "it was not really the eldest daughter, it was the second, but she was the first of the bunch to get married."

Her father and mother decided that it would be a good time to gather everybody, as many of them like Maas Josiah and Miss Elle had not seen each other for a long time. From as far away as Panama, relatives were coming. Miss Constance as usual was impressed. "Panama, you know Miss Bunchy, Panama, from cross the water."

"Relations you say coming?"

"Oh yes, mam," said Miss Conse, "blood relations mi dear mam."

Miss Bunchy was not as excited as her friend. "Well, mi dear, no so family stay – blood thicker than water."

"But to come all the way for a simple wedding is a wasterage."

"No mam," said Miss Bunchy, "the wedding is just the excuse, family want to meet with family and is a good

4

opportunity for them all to meet. Not a thing wrong with that. Dog have money him nyam cheese an flea have money him buy him owna dog."

And so it came to pass that the two weeks before the wedding witnessed the start of the arrival of scores of relatives from far and near, from "cross the water", as Miss Conse put it. And Miss Elle and Maas Josiah were among them.

The Sunday morning before the wedding, which was to take place on the Saturday of that same week, Miss Elle was in church looking as charming as ever. A darling of an old lady who had everybody astounded by her strong walk and sharp tongue, full of wit and humour. The next evening was to be the first family get-together for the early arrivals. The occasion was to be a moonlight hop on the big barbecue in Maas Roland's yard. Maas Roland was Maas Charley's brother. His cousin, Uncle Sam, with the violin and all the young men with banjo, guitar, fife and rumba box, were to play for the event. It was strictly by invitation and Maas Charley made it known that anybody who tried to enter without their invitation would be dealt with. But as everyone knew that Maas Charley was not a man you trifle with, there was no trouble.

Well, the occasion was grand, a good start to the wedding, and was the talk of the entire district for days. Uncle Sam and the fellows in the band played from quadrille to waltz to vaspiana, rumba to rags, and the people had a merry time. Young and old, all the members of the family and their friends danced and enjoyed themselves, putting aside all the little family squabbles and the big ones too for the night.

Miss Elle was chief among the dancers having a good time to the amazement of all and sundry. She had them all

wondering how this old lady who was supposed to be ninety was dancing up such a storm, putting many of the much younger ones to shame. In the middle of a polka, Michael, Maas Charley's son who was dancing with the old lady, felt somebody push him aside and take over. He turned around to see Maas Josiah. He politely stepped aside to give them room and Maas Josiah started to lick foot, with Miss Elle matching him step for step. Pretty soon everybody else stopped to watch the elderly couple as they were showing how the "polka really go." Miss Elle's still trim waist was making some movements that would do credit to her great grand-daughter. Many of the older folk called the young people to come and watch, to see "how polka dance". The musicians wouldn't stop playing and, as a matter of fact, were now challenging the dancers as much as the dancers were enticing them. It was a sight to behold. Everything else stopped and everybody was now focussed on the couple, clapping in time and urging them on. Finally the dance ended and the couple collapsed in each other's arms breathless. The applause and cheers were deafening. Josiah was beside himself, Miss Elle was as cool as a cucumber.

"Elle gal, a you?" he said unable to control his delight.

"Yes Josiah, a me same one," Miss Elle said fanning herself with a big straw fan that her grand-daughter had just handed her.

"My God," Josiah continued, "I can't believe it. Is a long time now you know and you don't change a bit."

"Massa you must be blind, a fool me woulda fool to believe that kind of foolishness."

"You know what I mean man. You looking good fi you age."

"That may be so, but a dog of my age is no pup."

"But you really looking good, is a good seventy year now we eye don't make four."

"Sixty nine years and four months to be exact," said Miss Elle, cocking her head to the side in the pose that always sent Josiah's blood boiling.

"My God, is true, and you know how long I did want to make a thing wid you."

"Oh, go away Josiah, you are an old man, make you age protect you....What kind of thing?"

"Oh come on Elle, you can't talk bout old you know, memba you older dan me."

Miss Elle stopped fanning. "So what dat have to do with the price of prementa." Everyone now realised that argument start and once more all eyes and ears were riveted on the couple.

Maas Josiah wouldn't allow Miss Elle to get away with anything, being a little bit of a show off. But he made the mistake of engaging her in a battle of words. Seems as if he had quite fogotten how sharp both her wit and tongue were.

"You memba say that when you was a big young miss, a breasted, me was a little boy inna first book – You older dan me by far," he said, relishing the moment.

"When it come to ole don't bother wid me you know Josiah, for as ole as me be you can't exercise me in no way, shape or form."

Josiah was now almost getting floored. He sensed that he was losing this brief engagement and made a desperate try to redeem himself. "Well my dear Elle," he said, pulling himself up to his full five foot six and a half, "you full a big chat as usual, maybe you should put you action where you mout be and take up the challenge."

Well Josiah was not prepared for what hit him next and left the party and the district in "disgrace" as he had no comeback to Miss Elle's parting shot. "You can say what you like for mout make a thousand drawers and backside don't wear one, when you ready to throw out you challenge, just you remember one thing." You could hear a pin drop as everybody waited to hear what Miss Elle was about to say. "Remember that all woman can lie dung but a no all man can tan up."

With that Miss Elle flounced off leaving Maas Josiah speechless, having to endure the howls of laughter that the crowd was now heaping on his embarrassment. However, he had the grace to admit that he was demolished.

"That woman is something else, she is the bestest."

And Maas Charley, being the perfect host, put his arm around Maas Josiah's shoulder and through his laughter said, "come Josiah, dat call for a drink, come we go take a whites."

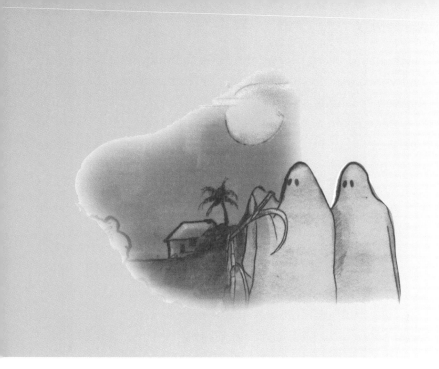

First Come — First Served

It was no secret Miss Zella had a special likeness for young men. The older folks whispered it, "Been doing it for years", and everybody in the district knew this. It was a source of great wonder and amusement for one and all. It was no secret also that none of the ones she chose to try out between husbands could cope with her, even though she was far older than all her assailants. She had a reputation for stamina, having buried three husbands to date and was on her fourth. She, however, behaved impeccably while each of her husbands was alive. Her activity then was confined strictly to suggestive comments, and plenty eyeballing. As soon as she was free, though, she went through the willing and sometimes not so willing young men like fire through cane-piece, using every trick in the book to bring them to her bed. She was the acknowledged trainer for the young men in the districts for miles around.

Take for instance after she buried Maas Butty, her third husband – he only lasted three years. Everybody said he was much too old for her. She was fifty-seven and he was almost seventy. He was, according to her reputation, bound to come to grief, and so it's said he did. He died of a heart attack trying to part two "man jackass" who had caught fight on the way from the railway one banana day and Miss Zella went on the rampage once more. It is said that the young men from far and wide were in a high state of excitement.

They all joked about whose turn it would be next and each secretly hoped it would be his turn next, or hoped it would not, depending on how each perceived his ability to cope with the legendary Miss Zella. For, according to Miss Constance, "is not one or two she disgrace." Many lost their prestige and boasted reputations among their companions as the strongest or the baddest or the best thing around. And plenty times in jest you'd hear them give their one another, "wait till Miss Zella ketch you", or "if you think you so bad or so good go challenge Miss Zella". There were some who, having over-estimated their own prowess, or under-estimated hers, would come away from the encounter, egos deflated or demolished to the amusement and derision of their friends.

A few, very few, succeeded in pleasing the lady however, so it is said. One of these was Leon, Mr. Curtis' youngest son, born after his first brother was all of twenty. He had the body of an athlete with muscles and chest like a pugilist, a big well-developed fellow who was reputed to be as gifted below the belt as above. He was living in Clarendon with his elder brother, learning the cooperage trade, and when he came back home at age twenty-two, he had all the girls going crazy for miles around and all the women in the village, young and old alike, secretly wishing that their husbands or boyfriends looked like him and could perform like his reputation said he could. And he had a field day playing the village ram. By the time he met up with Miss Zella one Saturday after market, she well knew about the reputation he had earned in the short space of time. Miss Zella was ready for the challenge.

Leon had gone to help his grandmother, Aunt Sophie, pack up the stall and take home the two big boxes of dry goods she sold in the market every Saturday right beside Miss Zella. As he approached the stall Miss Zella saw him. Her eyes opened wide, her skin "catch fire", and trying to hide the excitement she was feeling, she said to Aunt Sophie, "No you granson that, Curtis' bwoy?"

Aunt Sophie's two little beady eyes peeped over the gold rim spectacles as she replied, "Yes mi dear mam, him same one."

"Him look strapping and healthy like a bull," Miss Zella lusted.

"The old bitch," thought Aunt Sophie, "she must be think I don't know what she thinking." "Yes mam, strong and healthy fi true," she said aloud.

"Come here young man, I been hearing that you come back. I been hearing a lot about you." Miss Zella looked at him straight.

"Evening Miss Zella," Leon said, walking up to her. And from where Miss Zella was sitting her eye level was exactly in line with the bulge in Leon's tight "merican khaki" pants, and Miss Zella noted the weight with delight.

"You looking younger than ever," said Leon, "you don't change a bit, Miss Zella". They eyed each other.

"Well mi dear bwoy me tek care of miself, you know, and since Maas Butty gone, a just keep miself to miself," she said pointedly and Leon recognised the hint in her voice.

He too had heard of Miss Zella and he smiled to himself. "A wonder what it would really be like?" He had had his fill of the girls his own age and younger and a few older women, but none of them could exercise him. Take his latest encounter with Marjorie. As hefty as Marjorie was, she had spent the whole time whining about being hurt and begging him to stop. It was a waste of time. So he thought, if this old lady was as good as she was reputed to be, it could be fun. Leon then and there resolved to try her out for himself as soon as the opportunity presented itself. So while he was busy planning for Miss Zella, she was busy "baking bammy" for him. You know "old lady a swear fi eat callaloo and callaloo a swear fi run her belly!" Poor Aunt Sophie didn't know what to do. She couldn't say a word, though she knew exactly what her friend was thinking. She didn't dream that her grandson was himself making plans.

So the load was packed up in silence and when Leon picked up the two boxes and lifted them up on his head, stretching up, his frame further revealing his tapered waist and the power below that waist, Miss Zella nearly jumped out of her skin. "All right, Sophie, see you next week and Leon, you must come look fi mi one a these evenings when you come home from work."

"All right Miss Zella, one day," he said and he thought, "sooner than you think".

"Sneaky wretch," thought Aunt Sophie, "everybody know say Leon leave work after six so is night before him reach home. She no know say the Bible say you no fi put new wine inna ole bottle. Well sar, what a outa order women."

Leon was as anxious to visit as Miss Zella was to have him visit, and to cut a long story short, after that first visit three days later, he was a regular visitor to Miss Zella and the old lady walked with a spring in her step that astonished and amused everybody. She told Leon he was the best she had had in all her years. "You better by far than you puppa an him was one of the best. It must be run in the family."

Leon, under any pretext, visited Miss Zella regularly – to fix the gutter, the door hinge, the water barrel, the clothes line, you name it – maybe fooling everyone except Aunt Sophie who thought, "call it house-keeper, call it dressmaker, call it cook – is the same whorin".

Well less than two years later Leon got married to Girlie, Maas Percy's daughter from 'Merica and soon after moved to live with her in New York, Miss Zella was like fish out of water, but she kept quiet for a while. She was getting lonely and restless.

Talking to Aunt Birdie at market Miss Conse was heard to remark, "It will not be long she soon call egg again." True to form it wasn't for long. She was on the hunt again in no time, and it was not long after that she married again, this time to a man from outside the parish who had come as head farrier to the estate. He took one look at Miss Zella, she at him, and they both hit it off immediately. Well, tell the truth, as far as she was concerned, "any port in a storm". And either because she was getting on or he was a good husband, Miss Zella, to everybody's surprise, cooled down like a cucumber and was a model of modesty once more. The old people all sighed with relief as one of their number was returned to the fold of proper decorum and decency. "Well mam," said Miss Conse, "what don't happen in a year, happen in a day."

Things went well until that fatal Easter Monday when the truck carrying the estate cricket team just five miles away to a friendly cricket game, turned over on Union Hill Road and injured nine and killed one. The one? George Frankson, Miss Zella's husband. Poor Miss Zella, she cried her heart out, and the day before the funeral, it seemed as though Miss Zella herself would soon pass on. She cried non-stop and all her friends and family tried to console her to no avail. "Poor George, poor George, mi one George, oh, George dead! George gone, George gone!" The bawling would peak and lull, only to peak again with each new arrival at the house.

The old stories about Miss Zella's preferences and activities surfaced again, and all during the set-up, groups of young and old alike recounted the well worn tales of Miss Zella's escapades – of Claudy, Gerald, Mr. Burton, Percy, and Leon – and the tales went on. Needless to say, the stories, newly embellished, tickled the curiosity and raised the interest of the men in the district to a peak and the young swains jostled for her favours once more, some in jest, some in earnest, some daring to think they could gain the coveted prize, albeit more than a little worn, but nevertheless in their eyes, desirable.

Every single one of them admitted while they joked together that they were "afraid to try", or they "couldn't bother", or that they didn't believe what was being said was true. All and sundry said they would "leave well alone". That's why what happened the day of the funeral was such a big surprise, at least to one young man.

Mr. Frankson was buried beside the graves of the other two husbands in the family plot on the little rising above the coffee-piece (her first husband was buried in the churchyard) all during the service by the graveside that evening, according to Miss Constance, "Miss Zella mourn and weep, weep and mourn, for poor George" right till the last shovel full of clay molded up the grave and the headstone was put on and the red croton was planted at the head of the grave and the last shovel knocked.

Elder Palmer tried to console Miss Zella as did a host of other people, but Miss Zella wouldn't stop, and the wailing peaked again as she turned to leave the grave to go back through the coffee-piece up to the house. Nobody followed her because by now they were all a little fed up with the bawling and the carryings on. Many of the older folks ignored her and Miss Conse said, "Cho, is so she did gwaan fi di other three, it don't mean nothing." Everyone expected that if she ran true to form, it would only be a matter of time before she would find her solace in the arms and beneath the eager body of some strong young man.

Miss Zella went up the path through the coffee-piece, still weeping, "Lord, George dead! What mi going to do without mi George?"

Joslyn, Maas David's outside son by Miss Vie, who fancied himself a lady killer, coming down the path from the house, heard Miss Zella, "George, poor George", and the young man could think of nothing else to do or say to comfort the lady in her distress, so he put his arm around Miss Zella and said, "No mine, Miss Zella, no mine, I will come and keep you company tonight."

Poor Joslyn was in a state of shock for days, because through the wailing, "George, poor George", Miss Zella replied, "Oi, oi, somebody did ask mi already . . . Oh George! Poor George!"

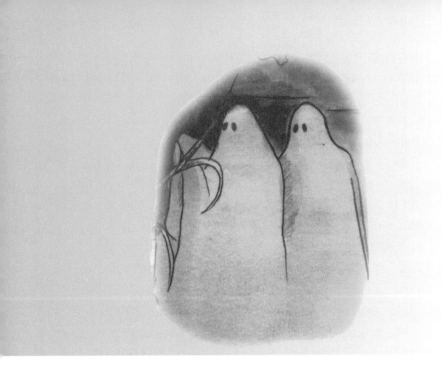

Let Brotherly Love . . .

When the two Chinese brothers arrived in Parker Piece to open their little shop, the villagers were very happy to have them, for before that they had to travel on the gravel road over two miles to Brighton to get their shop supplies or wait till Saturday when they would go to the market in the town eight miles away, and not everyone went to market.

The little shop was not more than about twenty by thirty feet but it soon had every imaginable item that the villagers needed. The stock ranged from basic bread, sugar, salt – fine and coarse – to pickled fish, stout, aerated water, common pins, hair pins, clothes pins, ready-made shirts, drawers, raw cloth, khaki and calico, poplin, satin and tobralco, salt physic, arrow root pills, black pepper, cornmeal and flour. They were also licensed to sell "rum, brandy, gin and other

distilled spirits". You name it, it was there. And if you asked for something and it was not there, you could bet next week it would be available, for they kept a list of all the items requested and made sure that the next time it would be included in their stock.

The two young men really fixed up the little shop. Everything was in order, neat and tidy, and when there was no customer to attend to, they were always dusting and fixing and rearranging to make sure everything was spic and span. Busha Parkins had built the shop out by the cross roads and it was said that it was he who had invited them to come. They were the nephews of his friend who owned the bakery in the market town. His wife also patronised the shop and there were some items that were specially brought because she requested them. Busha had rented the shop to the brothers at a reasonable rate, knowing that it would enhance the village and facilitate his workers. Almost half of the village workers were employed to the estate in one way or another in the cane fields, looking after the cattle and other livestock, or in the factory itself. The life of the village revolved around the estate.

The brothers, Albert and Charley, barely spoke the local language: they had arrived from China just six months before they came to Parker Piece, and in the early days business was conducted by making signs to their customers. They also kept a long stick the size of a broomstick but a little longer which the customers would use to point to the goods on the shelf to indicate their choice.

The brothers were very courteous, pleasant and mannerly. The whole village could see that they loved each other and they soon endeared themselves to the community. They were known to be strict businessmen, but had a reputation for dealing fairly and honestly with all persons.

No child ever went into the shop and left without a little treat. All the broken crackers and sweets were kept for them and they loved to "go to shop". Mother P was certain that every Friday she could get her stale bread which was kept for her as she couldn't eat the fresh one.

Both Albert and Charley were good carpenters. They had learnt the trade in China, and as time went on they helped to build and fix school furniture, and helped their new found friends to repair their houses, their windows and doors. Albert was soon to be acknowledged as the expert at hanging doors. They even helped to build the cedar coffins for the dead of the village, and when they helped with the repair and extension of the Church, benches and roof, and did such a good job, the Parson publicly thanked them for their help. "Today they prove that they are one of we." Soon the villagers were referring to them by their names, and not the accustomed "Chiney John". To really signify that they belonged, Granny Beckie the village matriarch now claimed them as her adopted. They referred to Miss Conse as Auntie.

They were well liked if not loved, and the little shop grew and prospered and they learned to speak the language, though there were still some words they could not pronounce correctly. When they were teased about this they, responded with the question, "You can talk di chiney lang?" Of course that provoked more teasing, but it was all between friends now.

The shop was doing so well that Busha had to extend the building twice in eight years. Even so, it was fast outgrowing the present building. They offered to buy the premises but Busha was reluctant to sell, and when a two acre piece of roadside land became available, at an attractive price, near the rail crossing about a couple of chains up the road, they quickly bought it and soon built their own upstairs building to expand the business. Now they had a private bar and added farm supplies to complement the farm tools they always carried. The dry goods section was expanded to include ladies hats and shoes for all, and they began to purchase produce, coffee, pimento, annatto and cocoa, on a large scale. At the back of the new shop they reared pigs and chickens, and planted vegetables the way they did in China. Auntie Conse was proud to say "Is me give them the callaloo seed you know and look here, as she displayed a nice bunch of fat greens.

Things were really booming for them. They worked hard six days a week, from dawn to late at night, and the only time off they took from working in the shop was on Sundays when they went to see their uncle at the bakery and played Chinese games with their family and friends. But no matter how late they came back on Sunday night, at the crack of dawn, bright and early Monday morning, the shop would be open. In a matter of ten years they were well established.

All this time they remained unmarried and unattached. Not that they lacked admirers. Many young women in the village and surrounding districts would have liked to be noticed by them and many tried by subtle and not so subtle means to attract them to no avail. Very often when they were asked by villagers about marriage the reply from both of them was always the same, "Lo leddy yet", or "Lo have money caan mallied."

However, the villagers noticed that both young men seemed to like one particular lady. She was the young sister of the Post Mistress, and was her assistant, and sometimes even acted for the PM when she went on short leave. Albert, the more outgoing of the two brothers, managed to convince her to leave the Post Office and work with them in the shop as they now needed help. Much to the dislike and upset of her sister she did, for she had a plan as she confided to her godmother, "If is not one it will be the other." Her godmother was pleased at the prospect and encouraged her, "Gwan mi chile, woman luck deh a dungle, an all yu need is a fowl fi scratch it out." So Belle came to work with the brothers who named the business Two Brothers Emporium, and had the name painted on the front of the building. The villagers, though, in typical fashion called it simply Two Brothers.

So now they employed a total of four persons, Belle and Miss Cass, who washed and cleaned for them and occasionally cooked the local food they had grown to like, Percy who looked after the animals and the garden and helped occasionally with the produce, and Harry the general handyman around the shop who fetched and carried and when the shop got busy helped to attend to customers, though he was not allowed to handle money.

It soon was common talk that Belle was liked by both brothers, and the guessing began as to which one as no one could tell and Belle was not saying. Some malicious persons expressed the opinion it was both, and that however it went she was a lucky girl. Belle became pregnant and the talk and the guessing intensified. They were sure it was one of the brothers, but which one. "Ah bet is Charley." "No Sir is Albert." "It could be both and we would never know the difference," Miss Conse was heard to laughingly remark. Maas Butty who knew everything said he was sure it was the quiet one Charley, for "the stillest calf suck the most milk". But he was wrong this time.

Albert did not know how to tell his brother that he was the father. But Charley knew, for he was not. A kind of tension developed between them as Charley barely spoke to his brother, only when absolutely necessary, though Albert tried to act as though nothing was amiss. After a few weeks and discussion with the Post Mistress, Albert decided to marry Belle and they began planning a simple wedding and asked Charley to help them, and stifling his hurt the brother said he would. Teacher Powell and Miss Mack, the village mother, were also asked for their help which they gladly gave and Albert was happy to see the tension between himself and Charley slowly lessen. When the wedding day came, Charley stood beside his brother as best man for the short ceremony in the church they had helped to repair. After the church, the small party of about twenty including Belle's relatives and a few choice friends repaired to the paved area at the back of the shop where they dried the produce. As it was Sunday there was no business.

y had spent all day Saturday and early Sunday reparing a delicious Chinese meal for the Miss Mack had baked and decorated a cake, and d Percy had made a coconut bow arch over the Drinks flowed freely and Busha took charge, ig several toasts to the couple. Albert's relatives who d to the marriage did not attend. His only support on de was his beloved brother Charley, and when he was I to say something, Albert said, "Me glad me mally good ian, she soon have baby."

erybody cheered as he continued, "Me happy all my good lens come to my celeblation, and best ting, me glad my blatda happy."

Forcing a smile, Charley nodded. When the festivities were over, late Sunday evening, Charley, assisted by Harry, Percy and Miss Cass, finished cleaning up so that by dusk there was very little if any evidence of the party except for the arch with the now limp flowers and croton that decorated it.

Things seemed to return to normal, as the brothers settled back in their routine. But Charley was quieter than before, avoiding his brother's and Belle's eyes. No one could know the depth of his hurt. He had really loved Belle but because he was so shy he had said nothing. As the weeks passed he did all the little things he had planned to do. He fixed the gutter at the side, completed the cement work around the paved drying area so the rain water would run off easily, and finished the work on the pig pen where the newborn and their mother sow were kept.

He had purchased a big-breed ewe goat and Harry was minding it "on increase" according to their agreement, and he now told Harry that he was making him a present of his share in the animal, so now Harry was the sole owner. Thinking it a little strange, Harry asked him what about the month old kids. "Them too," was the answer. Harry thought Charley was out of his head, but said nothing.

Charley left as usual to buy goods in town when the time came, telling his brother that he was also going to spend two days with their sister whom he had not seen for some time. In town, he went about his purchases as usual, saw to the loading of the truck and sent the driver on his way, "See yu few days time."

The days went by, and the weeks and the months, but Charley did not return. Now it was Albert's turn to hurt. He loved his younger brother, they had gone through so much together. Their boyhood days in China, the war when they faced death and starvation daily. The death of their parents, the days of hardship, the difficulties to get to his sister and uncle into this strange land. How they had looked after each other, Charley had even saved his life, and for those memories and the love of his only brother Albert in secret wept for days and nights.

And Charley too cried for his brother and missed him terribly. He was now with his sister and brother-in-law in her well established wholesale business, but nothing or no one could take the place of his brother.

As for Albert, only the arrival of his baby son seemed to cheer him up a bit and ease the depression that had settled on him. The baby was now his joy and pride, and as everyone observed, was the stamp of his younger brother Charley, and the name his father gave him, was Charley Albert Chin.

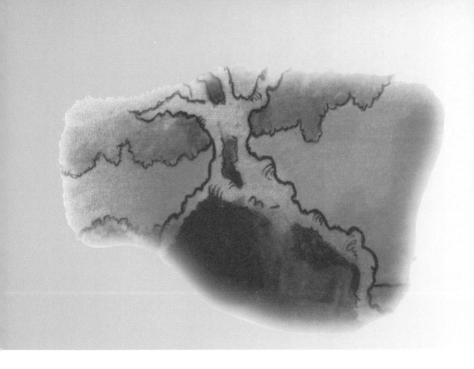

Push Start

The whole district was in an "upstir" as Miss Constance put it. Maas Tommy and Miss Edna were getting married. And as the date approached, the excitement grew. The stories about the details of the wedding were numerous, for this was no ordinary wedding. The couple had lived together since Miss Edna was age seventeen and had their first child and Maas Tommy's grandfather, Papi John, died and left him the four bedroom house on twenty-four acres, well fruited with eighteen heads of the best cattle. Miss Edna's mother "chaw fire" for years but Maas Tommy who was at that time twenty-two refused, for some strange reason, to marry Miss Edna. It seemed they both decided two things – not to get married and to have as many children as would fill the inherited house. And when the ninth was expected, he added two

extra bedrooms and to everyone's amazement a big bathroom, set up a pump system and six drums over the bathroom so that there was running water in the kitchen which was off the house, in the outside bathroom which was to the side of the kitchen and of course in the new inside bathroom with flush sewer – the first in the district.

You see, all this was possible because Maas Tommy was a strong hard-working man who didn't waste his money and his substance. And when other men were busy drinking and gambling and womanizing, he was at home with his cows, his pigs, his cane and food cultivation, his children and, of course, Miss Edna. So by all accounts he was a rich man. He had added to his holding almost a hundred acres and he bought a truck and a car.

The final count was fourteen children – seven boys and seven girls. And the talk was that everything Maas Tommy put his hand to, thrived and bore fruit, not least of all his wife, sorry his sweetheart, Miss Edna. That was the word for that kind of relationship in those days. That was the one thing that stood in the way of total respectability for this upstanding couple. Maas Tommy's children were all schooled and doing well but he and Miss Edna were still "living in sin".

He was fit and prosperous. Miss Edna was happy and bubbling. They had money. There was no reason why all these years they never married, at least none that anybody could see. Now in his fiftieth year, twenty-eight years later, Maas Tommy was ready for marriage. Miss Constance remarked, "Time longer than rope, and moon run till day ketch him. For if a me, me would lef him long time." But not Miss Edna. Her patience was legendary in the district and had become a proverb among those who knew her, so much so that in difficult situations the remark was often heard, "You need the patience of Job and Miss Edna together."

Miss Edna was a pretty young miss when she and Maas Tommy fell in love. She was the kind of young woman that turned heads and caused accidents and sleepless nights. Now at age forty-five, after fourteen children and eighteen grandchildren, she still turned heads. A little heavier, but the years had been very kind and according to old Lynch who had known her since she was born was fond of reminding her, she was still, "A haughty piece of flesh, enough to make a man sin."

Miss Constance had gathered the latest details about the plans for the wedding and as usual started to pass them on suitably embellished. But those plans were such that not even Miss Constance's wild imagination could fathom or surpass them. It was going to be a wedding to remember.

Miss Edna's daughters were to be bridesmaids, the seven of them, and all her sons, groomsmen. Chief Bridesmaid was to be Mrs. Farquharson, Miss Edna's teacher's daughter and her best friend. Bestman was to be Maas Tommy's cousin, Dr. Grant from Black River. The grand-daughters, twelve in all, were to be flower girls and the youngest grandson, ring bearer, the other five to be ushers to hand out programmes and escort the ladies to their seats in the church. "Is the first time in my born days mi ever hear say programme meck fi wedding," Miss Conse said. The church was to be decorated by Miss Irene and her assistants, Miss Pinny and Sister Jo. Mr. Bopsingh, the expert coconut bow plaitter, was in charge of arches. Busha Parkins was supervising the building of the wedding booth which would be fifty feet by fifty feet on the common beside the house.

"And mi dear, Miss Vie, mi hear say is one whole cow, six pig and six goat a go kill, and not to mention the fowl dem!"

"Say what Miss Conse?"

"What a feast!"

"And rice and peas, white yam, plain rice, plantain and fry dumplin, and show-bread and cake and liquor of all description!"

Miss Vie was mesmerised. "Lawd have mercy!"

Needless to say the information that Miss Conse was giving was grossly exaggerated. Nevertheless it was going to be a grand affair.

"Is four hundred people mi hear get invite – from all over Jamaica and 'Merica and Hinglan and Panama where im sister live," continued Miss Conse.

"Well mam, she deserve it," Miss Vie said, wiping a drop of eye-water from under the eye-glasses, "She wait long enough and work hard enough."

"So mi say too mam," agreed Miss Constance.

"Look at the amount of children she have and how she care him – Maas Tommy young as ever."

"And mi hear say him vicious you know mam."

Miss Vie was shocked. "Say what! But mi neva hear say him beat her."

"A no so mi mean, Miss Vie, you too simple." And with a wicked grin, Miss Conse whispered in her ear and the two dissolved in a gale of laughter.

"You too bad Miss Conse."

"No mam, morning, noon and night. As Brother Paul say the other day – six times a week and twice on Sundays – but I believe a envious him envious because according to the story, is constant drought at Spring Bump." They laughed louder.

"Well sir, you neva done," said Miss Vie.

"Well Miss Vie, mi hear say that him vicious to the point where if she a get ready to go out and him see her in her

underclothes, she have to satisfy him before she leave. You no see she never on time for anything yet. Always late and always the excuse is the children, for when she not busy minding them she busy making them or getting them."

"Miss Constance I only hope she on time for the wedding. Put fun and joke aside, I can't wait for the day to come."

"Me to," said Constance, "me don't get invite but me will be there at the church."

"I will see you for mi not missing it. Me reserve my place under the old pimento tree on the little rising between the school tank and the church so mi can see everything mi dear."

So the day came. It broke calm and beautiful. Not a cloud in the sky. Round about noon, a bank of fluffy white clouds covered the sun and followed it until evening, cooling down the whole place. The wedding was to be at four o'clock, but from early as two, people were gathering at the church to see the lovely decorations. The church was a beauty, flowers and ribbons everywhere – on the altar, in the sanctuary, in the choir stalls, the pulpit, on the benches – and the final touch came when the white and silver bell with the rice was hung on the plaited palm arch over the entrance and the two white satin ribbons to pull it open draped to the sides and temporarily fastened.

"Yes, this is out of this world," Miss Conse said, and all agreed. Similarly, the booth at the house was in beautiful readiness. The food was being given the finishing touches, and the servers were all waiting for the guests. The cake was a sight to see.

The *ten-cake* girls had taken four trips up to Mrs. Nash to bring all the cakes, including the six-story bridal cake. They had been provided with four different outfits and changed for each trip from pretty floral to crisp organdy

aprons over blue and pink and lavender dresses with trays decorated to match. That was only the prelude to the real wedding. With the show-bread covered up under the netting, the cakes were now waiting on the well decorated table for the bridal party to come from church.

By four, the church was almost full with guests, the churchyard equally full with lookers on, and the Bridesmaids, the Chief, the Bestman, the Ushers, the Groomsmen, Parson, everybody concerned, were all waiting for the arrival of the couple. Yes! The couple. This was unusual, for Maas Tommy had made the stipulation that the day he got married he was not sitting in the church sweating and waiting on his bride, for he didn't want what happened to his friend Frankie to happen to him.

Poor Frankie, as the story went, had proposed to a lady he had known only a short while and planned a big splash of a wedding. On the day of the wedding when he and all his guests were waiting in that same church, the lady didn't show up. At the time when she was supposed to be arriving at church, she was boarding the train at Appleton and was on her way to Montego Bay. Frankie nearly went mad. Maas Tommy who was his bestman had to console his friend. It was there and then he swore he would not be caught in that situation.

So, accordingly, the arrangement was that everyone was to proceed to the church and he would drive Miss Edna himself and meet them there and he would only wait long enough for the procession to be arranged from the back of the church – no more.

"Maas Tommy is a character though eh," said Teacher Spence as he waited with Manager and Custos at the church door. "But you have to lift your hat to the man though you know."

"Oh yes," the others agreed.

"I wonder why it took him all these years to decide to marry Miss Edna?" asked Custos.

"You never know. As far as we can see and know he has never had another lady, and there is nothing lacking in the relationship, but you never know, you never know. The Bible says Solomon, the wisest man, could not understand the ways of a man with a maid, you never know." That perhaps was the thought in everybody's mind that day as they patiently waited for the couple.

They were getting dressed about half a mile away between their home and the church at Maas Tommy's half brother's house. Both the brother and his wife arrived about twenty minutes ago, decked like everyone else in their wedding finery and said the couple would soon be there.

Well four o'clock came and went. No one was too upset as it was a bride's privilege to be late, but when ten minutes stretched to half an hour, to three quarters of an hour, to one hour, it was time to worry. People joked about last minute fright and that perhaps Maas Tommy had eloped with Miss Edna. One hour and fifteen minutes passed and J.P. Cousins, who was to be the master of ceremonies later, jumped into his old V8 Ford and set off down the road to see what was the matter.

Half hour later, and over two hours after the appointed time, the wedding march was being pumped out of the old pipe organ, and the most elaborate wedding ceremony the district was ever to witness was at last underway. And after the register was signed and the couple was out in the church yard receiving the congratulations and listening to their friends asking why they were so late, Maas Tommy just said that he had a little car trouble with his old Austin motor car. No sooner than that was fixed he discovered he had a puncture. So he had to take off his wedding suit, change the

tyre and bathe and dress again, and Miss Edna who was helping him had to do almost the same. Some believed him, some did not, others weren't sure. They asked questions such as "why he had to change the tyre himself, why Miss Edna had to help him on her wedding day of all days".

The wedding turned out to be the memorable occasion everyone thought it would be. Everything after the delay went according to plan and the wedding reception and dance continued well into the wee hours of the morning. The couple danced the bridal quadrille set and a few slow drags and waltzes, then the younger folks took over and food and drink and music were plentiful.

So the merriment and the fun continued with everyone having a grand time, forgetting the lateness of the couple. Only Miss Conse couldn't sleep. She was up the whole night still wondering if the car "did really puncture in truth or what, and how comes it couldn't start. What a coincidence. It don't look right – something did eena something."

J.P. Cousins was the only one who knew what the real reason was. For when he arrived at the house, as he didn't see anyone or hear anybody, he went right on the verandah, looked through the glass and saw everything through the lace curtain behind the sash window. However, as the true and loyal friend of the couple, he was saying nothing to any one. Later, however, when he was having a last drink with his old friend Busha Fenton, he made a telling remark without intention.

Both men were feeling more than a little tipsy, having had quite a few gins between them. Busha Fenton who was hard of hearing commented, "Imagine the blasted car refusing to start on the wedding day, what terribly bad luck."

"Yes, yes," laughed J.P., "had to get a push but that's one push start I would not have missed for anything. This time the laugh was quite lecherous.

Busha cupped his hand over his right ear. "Eh? What?"

J.P. continued his laugh. "Never mind, never mind, but it was surely the darndest sight to see."

But only he saw. As far as Maas Tommy was concerned, he knew that J.P. had seen everything. He was sure, however, that the day J.P. Cousins died, the secret went with him to his grave. That is why Maas Tommy could say at J.P's funeral when he was giving the eulogy, "He was my friend, faithful and just, and confidential to the end."

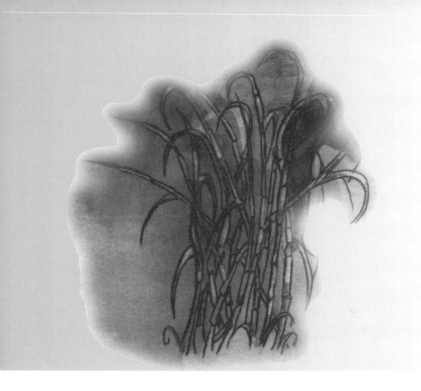

Strike

Maas Caleb wasn't too sure what to make of the story that suddenly burst upon him that quiet, cool, sunny afternoon. As was usual in the village at that time of day in this year of our Lord nineteen hundred and thirty-eight in the month of May, he was under the big breadnut tree near the roadside, to the side of the front of his place catching a snooze. As was customary, he had gotten up just before daybreak, according to Miss Conse "before cock put on him drawers". Maas Caleb was not unique in this, all his friends had the same routine; up before dawn, wash face, catch up fire, drink a cup of hot tea, coffee tea, cocoa tea, mint tea, bush tea or ovalstea and head to the "grung", chewing on a piece of hard dough bread or roasted yam and nothing was different.

Before the sun was up and hot enough to matter, say about nine or ten o'clock, a whole days-work almost would be finished. And so the men would rest till the afternoon sun had cooled sufficiently, and back to the field they went till evening, till brown dusk even, depending on the nature of the work for that day. Some things you just couldn't do in the half light. For instance, you could plant peas and corn, jam yamstick and tie bean vine on bramble, but weeding between the rows of tobacco, or peas or corn seedlings required full light.

Strange thing, though, no matter how soon-a-morning the women got up they didn't rest after lunch like the men. They had to make the lunch, cook the dinner, wash and clean. When the men went back to work in the afternoon, the women would be expected to stay home for house chores, the million and one things that house work demanded. So after the third mug of beverage (sugar and water and sibble orange), Maas Caleb was stretched full length under the breadnut tree on the two crocus bags, snoring, sawing board enough to build a church.

Coming down the road on the big mule-royal, Mister Young the village news bug was on the top of his voice calling out "strike, strike, strike". He was like a real newspaper. As there was no radio, newspaper seldom seen and the nearest telegraph office was over five miles away, he was the only means of passing news around. Parson or Busha Feddy would receive the news and tell Mister Young who had the job of going around from door to door, district to district, spreading the news, good or bad. Sometimes he took so long to get around that, according to Miss Conse, "The news grow junjo like stale bread."

Maas Caleb was angry and he was up like a shot cussing Mister Young for disturbing his peace.

"What the hell going on Puller?" The fact that he addressed Mister Young by his nickname signified the mood he was in, for Mister Young was older than Maas Caleb and commanded a certain respect.

"Strike, strike, strike awn. The whole island on strike, soldier and police all over the place."

"You damn ole fool, whey dat have to do with me," said Maas Caleb stretching out on the bags once more.

"Well, I don't know," said Puller, "but so I get i' so I sell i'. I am a no-profit news bulleteen," he said as he was off down the road calling out, and when he came to the village square he added, "Strike, strike, strike, lock up, a sudden lock up – lock up by four o'clock – strike, strike, strike".

Maas Luther took the warning seriously for he had travelled to Republic and knew about those things so he closed his doors and left the window open from which he could see out to the road. Miss Dassa, the other shopkeeper who was married to Mr. Chin You who kept his shop two miles away, wasn't so sure. She asked Mr. Young, "What you say going on Puller?"

"Strike mam, strike. The news say you must lock up by four o'clock. Riot in Kingston and riot in Frome a Wesmalan – a man name Bustamante leading them."

"What is the strike about?" Miss Dassa was asking.

"Well mam, ascordin to how it go dem want more pay. You better lock up yah mam, nuff soldier and police dey all over the place. Mi hear sey people a get beat up and dem kill a belly woman."

"When this happen?" Miss Dassa pressed him.

"Ah don't rightly know mam, Parson never tell me."

"But Mr. Young, we live quite een yah so, what dat have to do wid we." Like Maas Caleb, Miss Dassa was sure the strike in Westmoreland and Kingston was too far away to matter to them.

35

"My dear mam, I don't know but is so Parson tell me to warn everybody. Ascording to him, we should stay off the road, for plenty police and soldier up an dung."

"But quite yah so, how dat going to affect we?"

Again Puller pleaded innocence. "Well mam, mi don't know any more dan a tell you; effen you no believe me, den mi can't force you."

"What is all the commotion?" Miss Conse asked in her cruspy voice as she arrived on the scene. "I stay quite eena mi toilet and hear you mouth Mister Young."

"Him say strike on, Miss Conse," Miss Dassa said, "and that whole heap a police and soldier dey bout."

"Oh, Mister Young just letting off his mouth as usual, creating excitement. You remember the day him come tell mi sey..."

"Listen Miss Conse," Puller said, breaking his temporary silence, "I don't trouble you so puddung mi case, is your business what you want to believe, all I know is what Parson say to tell everybody so don't mel me."

Miss Conse would not be silenced so easily. "Oh go away you old idiot, you fooler than the old mule you riding, I suppose we soon see soldier an police coming up the road."

By now a few more people were gathering around; Maas Purcell, the wooden foot man Josh, Maas Casbert and Teacher Powell, and they were all discussing this latest piece of news. Some felt they were too remote from the reported centres of the strike activity, some said they had heard that over a thousand people were shot down by the white soldiers from the camp in Kingston and one man reported that his sister-in-law who arrived by the mail van from Mandeville had said that a pregnant woman was cut open with a bayonet so that her unborn baby was exposed.

Teacher Powell tried to calm everybody and encouraged them all to go back home and stay off the road, at least they would be out of harm's way. Mr. Ankle who was half drunk as usual insisted that he was going no further than "Mr. Mack bar" – as far as he was concerned, the strike had nothing to do with him and he had nothing to do with any strike and Puller was "a damn mischief maker". Teacher said you couldn't be too sure and that because they were not so far from two sugar estates, with the farthest one less than twenty miles away, they should take heed. Since the trouble was on a big sugar estate it just might mean that all sugar estates could have some problems. Miss Conse agreed, but then she always agreed with Teacher, for Teacher was "edicatid".

Mr. Ankle, swaying and slurring under the whites, said, "With reshpects Teacher, that is foolishness. Nexcht thing you going tell me shay you agree with Puller and that we shoon see lorry load a sholdier marching up the road."

It was as if he had seen them, for no sooner had the words left his mouth, the sound of heavy vehicles was heard coming up the road. The little crowd watched in stunned silence as two soldier lorries stopped across the road right in front of Miss Dassa's shop and the white soldiers alighted immediately. Two little boys, Percy and Man Man, were about to make a run when the soldier who seemed to be in charge said, "Don't run lads, we're not going to harm you. We are just a bunch of hungry soldiers looking for something to eat."

Well, in less than no time, the thirty soldiers consumed all the bread and bully beef and sardine and other tinned things in the tiny shop and drank out all the aerated water and wanted more food. Miss Dassa said, "The only thing we have is the corn in the field and plenty breadfruit." Before you know it, breadfruit pick, corn bruck and a big fire was blazing in Miss Dassa's yard beside the shop. Quantities of roast corn and roast breadfruit and salt butter were being devoured by the white soldiers from Kingston while the villagers watched in amazement, some remarking, "Look how di white man dem a get dung eena di breadfruit"; "Me neva know mi woulda live fi si this"; "After dem no better dan breadfruit"; "When man inna trouble pickney clothes fit him doh eeh".

"Sometime you haffi take shame face and shake coco bay man han." That was Mister Young as he tied up the mule on the little cedar tree near the side of the shop.

As it turned out, the soldiers were on guard at Appleton and Raheen Estates and were on their way back to camp in Kingston when they took a wrong turn and ended up in Comfort, miles away from where they should be. The strike was long over and the news Puller was giving out was over a week old. The villagers didn't know that, and for this sleepy village almost in the middle of the island, it was like a holiday. Teacher, Puller, drunk-already Mr. Ankle, and Miss Conse were all helping to feed the soldiers and chatting them up. Miss Conse helped Miss Dassa mix a doona pan full of beverage and the laughter and chatter soon broke out into song. The soldiers sang and made merry while the astonished villagers enjoyed the excitement. And when they started singing "Coming through the Rye", Miss Conse was in shock. "Imagine dem know mi ole school song doh eeh, Miss Dassa," and joined in harmonizing the last line, "When coming through the Rye", she sang her heart out.

"Ye know this ditty lass. What a grand surprise," the tall red head soldier said, hugging Miss Conse. The two of them dissolved into laughter having surprised each other and

sang to their hearts content – "Every laddie has a lassie coming through the rye, if a body kiss a body need a body cry."

Hours later after handsomely rewarding Miss Dassa, they drove away leaving Puller to enjoy the apologies being heaped on him by the doubters among his friends. Mr. Ankle who sought any excuse for a drink put his arm around Mr. Young, "Come Puller, you were right thish time. You deserve a whites. Come mek we take a whites, thish calls for a whites."

Free ... Free ... Free

We sleep wi dream wi eat wi drink ...free...
We work wi toil wi sweat wi think ...free...
We laugh wi chant wi dance wi sing...free...
We pray wi plot wi plan wi scheme
Ongle one blessed ting
Free...free...free...

Backra gi wi Bible fi tame wi
An meck wi more tractable an calm
Im say wi lazy an fool fool
For im tink wisdom an learnin
Only come under fi him skin
Or outa fim him language one
Das why im teck whey fi wi own? a wonder
Dung to wi very drum
But wi only play fool fi ketch wise.
An im no falla wha Bible teach
Im no do what im alsway a preach.
An im tink wi nah look
But wi read the whole blessed book
From the beginning till wi reach di en
Him tink is a big big joke
"From cover to cover every ruddy word, poor bloke"
The whole tick book full a di livin trute
An is the trute whey meck yu free
Free...free...free...
In between di page dem
wi fine a warrior powerful an mighty
Stronger more dan any soldier army, a fren

To company wi to di en of the journey
Who give im life fi set wi free
Free...free...free...
Though the road is tough an long
Wi keep di fate an wi nah stap pray
An as wi journey wi sing dis ya song
"Some day some day I"ll go where Jesus is
Some day some day...
An wi have di backitive and strent
From wi old people wisdom.
One day one day Congo tay.

So di day come di journey en
At laas wi free...free ...free...free...
An what a joy dat was fi all a wi
Who live long enough fi seet
Missis Queen sign a sheet a paper
Soh say she gi wi free
Ka nana po
Nutten no go so Ka nana po
Wee know what is di whole trute, di livin trute
Wi free yes wi free...free...free
But a noh she...ah wee
Wi fait wi sweat wi blood
Wi eye water wi cunny wi strent
Wi very life....
An wi trus an prias to the jus Almighty
Soh no meck nobaddy gwan tell yu dat lie
No one nuh gi wi nutten fi nutten
Meck yu pickney dem know it
Is wee...weeself...wee....
A fi wi owna struggle earn fi wi free...free...free...

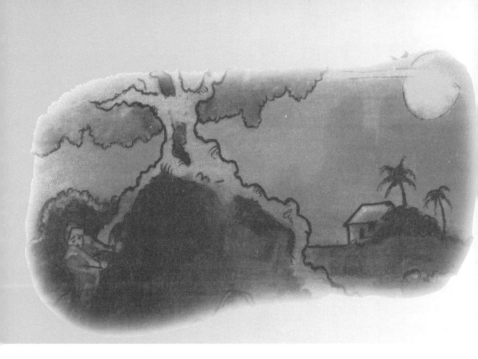

There is a Time . . .

Miss Constance was really "vex". No one had ever seen her so angry. And she had every reason to be. Matter of fact she was not the only one. Unusually, many people shared her views and she, knowing she had support, was encouraged and did not hesitate to make her feelings known all over the village.

"Is a damn disgrace!" Miss Constance was on the post office steps and a crowd was there waiting for office to open. "Imagine the jury find him not guilty and everybody including the judge know him guilty as hell."

Maas Luther was trying to reason the thing out. "But the jury find him not guilty," he said, appealing to those around him.

Miss Constance flew into a rage because of that remark. "Which jury, Maas Luther? So so man, the whole of dem would do the same thing and nobody don't tell me that seven man would convict another man for raping a woman and not guilty no mean im innocent. Me don't care what unno want to say, the whole of dem would do the same thing. Everybody know that Joslyn cut the throat and no man from earth to heaven could a tell me otherwise. Jesas himself would have to come offa the cross and tell me so, that's the only way I could believe."

Mother P agreed with her. "You see, Miss Conse, the only way him would be convicted for that offence, that is if the jury was woman jury."

Maas Luther laughed. "Where you ever hear that woman a turn juror?"

The case under discussion was the charge of rape that had been brought against Joslyn, one of the young men from the village. It was a difficult case: although he had a reputation of getting what he wanted from the girls he fancied, the judge had said there was a difference between raping a woman and forcing her to give in. This he explained to the jury and then said that the evidence showed that the victim gave in and in the final moments consented. Well that is what he said but everybody knew how Joslyn operated. It is true that he never held up anybody with a knife or any other weapon but he used all kinds of means to get what he wanted.

Joslyn was a peculiar young man. He was very attractive, had a good build, and was handsome. To look at him you would think he is the sort of fellow that you wouldn't mind if your sister was along with. But ever since he was about eighteen he had a funny streak. He only wanted the girls that didn't want him. He had his fair share of the women in the village and around. It was no secret there were girls and women who were after him and would give anything to get him. But he paid them no mind. He only wanted the ones who ignored him. He used all manner of trickery and duress to bring them to his bed. This had gone on for five or so years and so everyone knew the story. He always got what he wanted and managed to steer clear of the law till now.

Some of the ruses he used were quite amusing. For instance, when he wanted to get Miss Fan's daughter Florence, he told her that the severe headaches she was having were due to the fact that at twenty she was still a virgin and that she must do it "regular" or it would fly up in her head and make her mad. He couldn't or didn't say what would fly up, but Florence believed him and so according to him took several doses of the medicine that he prescribed. When the headaches persisted and she finally saw a doctor, it was discovered that she had a bad case of sinusitis, but the damage was already done. He told Betty Jenkins a similar story when she had cramps in her abdomen during her period, and the stupid girl believed him and ended up pregnant for him. Those were relatively harmless ruses because they were fairly easy cases to make. The more difficult the case, the more serious his ploy. Take the time when he seduced his cousin Patricia. She was just past fourteen. Her cousins from town had come to visit, including Sang, the son of their Aunt Cassy who married a Chinese man. For many months Joslyn had been after Pat and she had stoutly resisted him. The more she resisted the more he pressured her and tried to seduce her. She knew what she wanted and it was not to go to bed with Joslyn.

Well this day, while her cousins were visiting, her grandfather sent her to go across the road over to bottom yard to her uncle's house to call him, and she and her cousin Sang took off at a speed. They ran across the road, crossed the narrow level and headed down the hill to the house. Just as they reached the drain at the foot of the little hill, she realised that they would have to jump and that perhaps Sang couldn't make it, so she grabbed his hand calling out, "jump". Together they soared into the air over the drain laughing, still holding hands, and as they landed on the other side of the drain they fell, rolling over each other in the guinea grass patch, laughing and enjoying the fun.

When they got up and were about to continue on the path to the house, they noticed Joslyn standing on the rise above them over the other side in his father's yam garden. He too was laughing. On their way back from delivering the message, Joslyn called Pat to come to him and she left the path and walked through the grass to where he was standing, stripped to his waist, the message of his body language coming loud and clear. Moments later, Pat left him and went back to her grandfather. For weeks Joslyn kept up the pressure until in her absolute fear Pat gave in to him for he had threatened to expose her to her grandfather. He claimed that he had seen her and her little cousin, barely nine years old, "doing it" in the grass and that if she didn't give him his share he would tell. Poor Pat was scared out of her wits and he tormented her till he got what he wanted. She was lucky not to get pregnant.

So Joslyn went on with his wrongs and all after the trial his acquittal gave him new impetus and he was bolder and more open than ever. He boasted that no one could stop him. His friends, who usually relished the stories he so freely told of his conquests, were more than concerned. They were becoming embarrassed by the barefaced way he spread the stories of his exploits and went about his wicked plans to seduce the young girls of the village. Not even Mother P's pleadings and warnings made any difference to Joslyn. "Joslyn, you have to stop this wholesale slaughter, it not right," said Mother P.

"Cho old lady you just jealous because I don't come look for you."

The old lady was outraged, "Kir out bwoy, you no man enough for dat, you think because you a walk an destroy all the young gal dem, you think you a man, but mark my word, you gwine come to a bad end, or me don't name Priscilla Newman. "Renkas!"

"Well from he said that to Mother P that day all his friends shunned him and as they isolated him he became more and more vicious.

It was no doubt because Mother P had humiliated him that he next turned his attention to her two grand-daughters, Maas Butty's twin girls who were about fifteen years old. These two lovely girls, Violet and Jasmine, were the apple of their grandmother's eye. Their mother had died giving birth to them and their father had never remarried. He migrated to the United States leaving them with his mother. They were to join him as soon as they were out of school and would finish their education in America. Violet was very bright and she was expected to become a lawyer. Jasmine on the other hand, according to Teacher, was considered not as bright in school but what she lacked in brains she more than made up in looks and attractiveness. Her skin was dusky brown and she was smooth and pretty. She was not only pretty in face and body, her sweet and loving disposition was well known and admired by young and old alike. She was a truly lovely girl.

Joslyn was afire for Jasmine. And as was to be expected she didn't notice him. And the more she ignored him the more he wanted her. It was like an obsession with him. But he knew he had to be careful, so he bided his time.

It is strange how sometimes things work for the wrong doer against the innocent and unsuspecting. As Miss Conse remarked after the incident, "The devil seem to work overtime when the guardian angel dem a doze off."

It was the height of the rainy season one October month. Jasmine rode her bicycle to the nearby village to visit a sick relative. It rained so much that they tried to persuade her to stay the night. However, she decided to chance the journey back home and just as it was getting dark she reached the bridge, only to find that the water had started to come over into the road. Without thinking of the danger, she tried to cross, and in a few moments it was clear that she was in trouble. As the water swept her away she let go of the bicycle and the bag she was carrying and clung to the bridge rail calling for help. It seemed an eternity as she clung desperately to the rails not daring to move. She was sure she was going to be washed away. She shouted as loudly as she could.

The water was now above her waist and she was on the verge of panicking when she saw him emerge from the shadows coming across the water with one hand on the bridge rail. As he reached her he turned around and said, "Climb up pon mi back." Jasmine was so happy and thankful to be rescued that she did not then notice that it was Joslyn. He took her safely to the edge of the cane field where there was a makeshift hut left there by the canecutters and where they could at least shelter. He retrieved the bicycle but the bag was washed away. What took place in the cane field while rain and thunder and lightning raged was to be expected. And after that Jasmine was never the same again. She told Mother P the story and of course Mother P went to

Corporal. Jasmine swore out a statement and Joslyn was once more before the court, charged with carnal abuse, for Jasmine was under age.

The whole village was sure he was going to prison this time. Everyone thought that there was no way he could escape, this was plain and straight. To their surprise and annoyance, once more Joslyn was found not guilty. The old judge was not in sympathy with these "loose girls who throw down themselves in front of every man" and insisted that if they continued in their unseemly behaviour, then there would always be men to take advantage of the situation. "After all, men were men." What's more, he made it clear that he believed Joslyn's story that Jasmine was simply paying him for having rescued her from certain death. Miss Conse had to bite her tongue not to give him a piece of her mind a week later when she saw Judge coming out of church after J.P. Rhoden's funeral.

Jasmine was as if she had gone out of her mind. She wouldn't eat, she stopped going anywhere. She didn't go to church, nor school, nowhere. Not even to the gate, and she even stopped taking care of herself. She just sat day after day in the house, crying and not speaking to anyone. Poor Violet was distraught. Her sweet sister was like a lunatic, and all because of Joslyn. When a few months had passed and there was no improvement in Jasmine's condition, even after she had seen the doctor many times, Mother P took her to a balm yard in St. Elizabeth. The lady in charge of the balm said she couldn't do anything for her, and when Violet heard that, she decided that Joslyn had to pay. How, she was not sure, but she swore she would find a way to avenge her sister.

It was so surprising to everyone that while most people in the district despised and isolated Joslyn for his beastly act, Violet was one of the few who spoke to him, and poor Miss Conse couldn't understand what was happening.

"See here Miss Vie, me don't understand these young people. Imagine, I was coming up Spring Hill a while ago and who a buck up but the Miss Violet she, a chat up to the Joslyn him as good as ever. Bwoy who wreck her sister life and turn her in a idiot. Well done."

But Violet had a plan and when her grandmother accosted her about her action towards Joslyn, all she said was, "Cho Granny P, it don't mean nothing. After all, maybe Jasmine was up to it." The old lady couldn't believe her ears, "You must be mad, next thing I am going to hear is that you going to be sleeping with him."

Violet said nothing so as not to prolong the discussion. But she knew then what she was going to do. The old lady had provided the answer.

Violet laid her plan carefully. If she appeared too interested, Joslyn would ignore her. She had to pretend not to want him, yet at the same time send the right amount of signals to entice him. Her chance came when she was asked to perform in a school concert and she decided to wear a dress belonging to her sister and to dress up as much as she could to resemble Jasmine. That wasn't hard – they resembled each other, were almost identical. Well it worked like a charm, and after the concert that night, Joslyn was buzzing around like bees around honey. Violet gave him enough encouragement, just enough, and then when he made his move she let him know that she was not interested. Joslyn was becoming obsessed by the idea of this new seduction, and Violet played with him like a cat with a mouse. He didn't even suspect that this she-cat was just waiting for the kill.

Her chance came one evening when she was alone at home. Mother P had gone to Mandeville with Jasmine for the week and her cousin Bella, who stayed with them, had gone to Balaclava to the dentist and wouldn't be coming back before evening on the train. As luck would have it, coming home from the post office, who should she see walking up ahead of her but Joslyn. She hurried up the hill to her grandmother's house and passed him as he stopped to talk to Old Jackman, the wooden foot man who sometimes worked for her granny. As she passed she said, "Evening Jackman, evening Joslyn."

They both replied and for Joslyn's benefit she said, "Jackman, Granny P said to tell you that you must leave the coffee till she come back next week".

"Yes Miss V, Bella tell mi this morning already."

"You know Bella gone to Balaclava to pull out teeth that is giving her trouble."

"Yes I know," Jackman said.

"She didn't sleep last night," Violet said, and Joslyn took the bait. He thought, "she alone at the house, well this is mi chance."

He could barely wait till she disappeared up the hill to say goodbye to Jackman and start off up to the house. Violet was inside her room. He peeped through the window and saw her taking off her clothes. Unknown to him, she had watched him from behind the curtain as he turned into the path off the road and she knew he was watching her. She took off her dress and slip and was standing in her panties provocatively stroking her breasts under her thin brassiere.

"The little bitch in heat, green guava deh yah fi cool yu!" he thought as he pushed the door open.

Violet turned around pretending that she was about to scream, and Joslyn said, "No, don't make no noise, nobody

will hear you anyway and a not gwine hurt you, just take it easy." He closed the door behind him.

Violet was ready for him, "Hurt me? You think you can hurt me? It take bigger man than you fi hurt me."

"How you mean?" he asked.

"Well me handle bigger than you already."

"Gwan, you can't fool mi, you no look like you ever dweet yet."

"Gway yah bwoy, me handle some big man already, from me thirteen me a dweet wid big man," she lied.

"Call one man name you dweet wid already."

Again she lied, "You remember Teacher Grant? Well him and Maas Victor from Maggotty."

Joslyn was surprised, these two men were reputed to have the biggest privates anyone had ever seen. Violet had heard the stories too and chose these names for the very reason. She looked into his eyes and smiled.

Joslyn was now throbbing with desire, his hand found his erection bulging in his pants. "Then take off the trousers no," Violet said, "mek a see if you have anything".

In a flash, Joslyn was out of his pants advancing to her, unable to control himself, his erection now fully exposed as his underpants fell to the ground. He reached for her panties and quickly started to pull them off, seeing or hearing nothing. Equally quickly, Violet whipped the one sided razor blade she was hiding in her plait and with one deft stroke sliced him right across his erected shaft. Before Joslyn knew what happened there was blood all over the room and he screamed in pain.

Grabbing up his trousers he yelled, "You bitch you, I gwine bruck you rass neck, you little dutty rass!" His hands were now filled with blood. He took her blouse from off the bed and tried to stop the bleeding. "I gwine kill you blood cloth, you dutty hore."

Violet by this time picked up the kitchen knife she had hidden on the table in the corner of the room.

"Come meck we see who gwine kill who today. You think is today a want to fix you business for what you do to mi sister, you old jancrow. Get youself out of this house before I call dung crowd pon you today. You lucky I didn't cut it off all together, den I see what you would use to spoil up people gal pickney."

Joslyn knew he was defeated. He was still bleeding and terrified. He managed to get on his pants, but he was unable to prevent the blood from messing it up good and proper. As he edged his way out of the room with Violet menacing him with the knife, he said, "I gwine straight to the police station and make them lock up yu backside".

"Yes, tell them how it go, tell them how you follow me into the house and tried to rape me, tell them how you come by the cut, carry the evidence go show dem, and see who dem lock up today."

Joslyn who had intimidated so many people was now totally cowed. He ran from the house, but instead of going to the station he went to beg Teacher to take him to the doctor. He couldn't tell Teacher the truth, he told him he had an accident while he was sharpening his cutlass.

Joslyn was totally subdued after that. He molested no one and withdrew from everyone, living by himself on the little hillside of rockstone owned by his father. He became what Jasmine was – a mental case – for it was said that though the doctor could heal the wound he was unable to restore Joslyn's manhood and he never had another erection after that. When the story came out as all stories do, Miss Conse was beside herself with delight. "Well mam, she deserve a medal, wicked wretch, him coatie cut." Joslyn had not even gone to the police station so no charges were made against Violet.

Bull Muma

Parson was happy, he said, to announce to the full church that the new Governor on tour of the island was coming to visit the village in three weeks time. The whole congregation greeted the news with expressions of pleasure and delight, and after service they gathered up in little groups to begin to talk about the coming event as if it were the biggest thing that would ever happen to them. But so it was in that village, the slightest thing was a major happening, and indeed this would be the first time in the history of the village that anything like that had happened.

"Governor, Miss Gerty," said Miss Conse in amazement from behind the hymn book held at the side of her mouth to hide the fact that she was talking in church, and Miss Gerty nodded, "Hmm, hm!"

Parson had said he was happy that on his tour of the island the new Governor had chosen their village as one of his stops, and that they would need to meet to see what was to be done, who was to do what and he was asking for volunteers. The first meeting was tomorrow evening at five o'clock, and he expected a good turn out. He would see to it that the meeting didn't last until dark, for since it was war time, he didn't want to keep them long. He wanted everybody back home before night fall.

"Imagine you can't go about your business as you like, eh Miss Gerty, because of this Hitler and him damn foolishness," Miss Conse said.

She was sure Hitler was the devil incarnate. That was one of the hardships of the war. People stayed off the streets at night because air raids usually took place then and everyone tried not to have too many lights on. The big scout campfire had to be cancelled, for the villagers were sure it would attract German bombers.

"Just last week Tuesday me hear plane flying whole night over we and me just out the lamp and the fire in the yard where I was cooking the hog feedin. You can't take the chance," said Mr. Foster, the signal man at the railway crossing.

The blackout at nights, for some strange reason, was the thing that most annoyed Miss Conse, and as usual she made her feelings known. "That viper, because of him, me quite ya so is inconvenience."

"Well Miss Conse, is so the world go, the innocent always suffer most," Miss Gerty consoled her.

"But you know Miss Gerty, all the shortridge no bother me for as you know we grow wi owna food, things like gas and motor car is for Busha and dem rich people fi worry bout, but this darkness; quite a Jamaica ya so dis cantankerous man making wi life miserable, but God nah sleep, me can manage and Hitler can stay there wid his wickedness, you mark my words, he will come to a sad and bitter end. Time longer dan rope."

It's as if Miss Conse didn't experience dark nights as a regular feature of village life.

"Well Miss Conse, we can't stop that, but we have to go to the meeting tomorrow and see what we can do," said Miss Gerty.

"Yes mam, true," Miss Conse agreed, "see you tomorrow".

Well, the meeting was a success, plenty people turned out. One group was to decorate the school yard, one to see that the village square was cleaned and the stones white-washed. The children were to be asked to clear up the school yard and to practice special songs to sing at the occasion. "Rule Britannia", "Welcome Weary Traveler", "God Save The King", and "My Bonnie Lies Over The Ocean" were to be rehearsed and rehearsed to perfection, and two children were to be selected to recite. Uncle Sam and the village band were to play on the steps of Mr. Rob's shop facing the school gate, the scout drum band to play at the crossing. Everybody had a task.

Since they would be stopping first in the nearby town, they would have had lunch before they got to Comfort, so all they would be offered was a cool drink. Now the big decision had to be made, where was it to be served. After much wrangling and debating and going and coming, the meeting decided that they would be offered the drink at the end of the visit at Mr. Simpson's house down by Bottom Pond on their way out of the village. The visit was to last about an hour and the party was bound to be thirsty by then. As Miss Conse remarked, "English people can't stand heat!"

Miss Bell, Mr. Simpson's sister, who lived with him said it would be all right, she would see to it. She had the necessary wares and utensils, and as the whole village knew, she was the only one who was so equipped. She had spent many years in Panama and brought home all those things, from a pin to an anchor. She also informed the meeting that Police Inspector Nembhard was their cousin and that he had sent a message to say that he was one of the Officers accompanying the Governor. This news delighted everyone. Parson thanked her and said it was an amazing coincidence.

Of course, Mr. Simpson was the most delighted of all, and he revelled in the prospect of the visit. He lived in a modest but pretty little country cottage, with fretwork and lattice verandah, situated on about two acres. He was a retired farmer, and spent all his time looking after his pretty garden, his pride and joy. It was a show piece. You really couldn't find a prettier spot. It seemed the ideal place. The four cows would be moved way round the back so the cars could park on the common in front of the house and the garden with the big pink cassia tree in full bloom, and the "different colour" June rose right round the inside fence would be very pleasing.

Miss Bell had promised to provide coconut water, orange juice and lemonade so they could have a choice and as they were expected to offer about a dozen people a drink, she would prepare for twenty, to make sure she had enough. Miss Conse who was always pushing up herself, looking for an opportunity to show the rest of the ladies the "prapper way" to do things, volunteered to help. Miss Bell was not too anxious to have Miss Conse causing any confusion – "This woman is like coconut she's in everything," she thought – so she gracefully said she and the home folks would be able to manage for she had a servant girl.

She gently refused the offer in her most charming and diplomatic manner. "In any case Miss Conse, you should be enjoying the visit and not have to work this time – you always working".

Miss Conse basked in the flattery, little suspecting that Miss Bell didn't want her around for she had the reputation for taking over situations, and on such an important occasion there would be none of that. This was a once in a lifetime opportunity for Miss Bell to prove something she always wanted to, that she was by far the only female in the village who knew how to accommodate and entertain important people, and she was the only one who had the linen, glassware and other utensils to provide for such officials like Bishop and Governor. She could accommodate the King and Queen if need be.

Well, by the time the officials came, there was much talk and confusion. Mr. Williams said he was sure that was how the Tower of Babel must have been. Yet despite that, the visit went like clockwork. Though Parson took the credit and had lead the local planning, the success was due to the fact that the police and soldiers took everything under control and everybody, including Parson, Busha, Teacher and Custos, had to abide by what they said.

The Governor and his Lady were met at the school yard with the big Union Jack fluttering from a tall straight bamboo pole planted near the school. The children, smartly turned out in freshly washed, starched and ironed uniforms (girls in middi blouse and skirt, boys in khaki short pants and shirt) lustily sang "God Save The King", waved their little paper Union Jacks, and dutifully smiled from faces carefully washed and scrubbed for the occasion, now glistening with the beads of perspiration the midday sun brought out.

They sang "Welcome Weary Traveler" and the Governor was very pleased. And if the Governor was visibly pleased, the children were more than happy, not because the Governor was visiting, but really because as soon as he left, they would have the rest of the day off, almost the whole day, and then the cricket and the rounders would start. With this in mind, when they were asked to sing again, they sang with all their hearts, "When Bound By The Red, White and Blue".

The village shops all put up welcoming signs. One had a giant 'V' covered with ferns, asparagus vines and poinciana blossoms and red, white and blue strips of cloth. This one caught the eye of the Governor as he walked past. Beaming, he said aloud, "Wonderful, splendid, V for victory, so appropriate in these times," and he held up his hand showing the two finger V sign, and all the bystanders, mostly adults dressed in their best, lining both sides of the road, responded likewise and cheered and clapped.

One man, a veteran of World War One, had a letter he wanted the Governor to deliver to Mr. Churchill in England. The Police Inspector took it and gave him a solemn promise that Mr. Churchill would get the letter at the earliest opportunity. Solgie was gratified, "After all, I want Mr. Churchill to know that I am behind him and ready to fight again". So saying, he came smartly and suddenly to attention and saluted to the amusement of the crowd. He had written to Mr. Churchill, and among other things, said he had at least thirty soldiers from the First World War who had fought and thrashed the Kaiser, ready to administer a dose of the same medicine to Hitler, his forward hurry-come-up cousin, this despite their age and stage.

When he made his speech, the Governor thanked everyone and said he had not seen such a spirit of good will and determination and courage. He was sure the

community would prosper and that Great Britain, with the help of God and such villagers, would win the war and conquer the enemy, thus defeating evil. He would be sure to report what he had experienced on that day to the Colonial Office, who would in turn advise His Majesty that he had found in Jamaica, loyal and law abiding subjects. The crowd cheered heartily and burst into song, singing lustily, "Rule Britannia, Britons Never, Never Shall Be Slaves". Barda in his deep rumbling bass voice intoned "never, never, never" for almost five minutes.

The Governor's wife met and shook hands with the ladies of the Mothers' Union and Dorcas Society members. Miss Conse, in the purple lace and velvet dress she got from her sister in Cuba, curtsied and couldn't come back up, and if Mr. Beal didn't assist her, she would have fallen flat on her bottom. The children and the adults giggled at the sight. The "Lady Governor" or "Missis Governor", as she was called by some of the villagers, viewed the hand-work and cooking display they had put out specially for her. She tasted the grater cake, and as was expected, said how delicious it was. She had never tasted anything like it before. She even advised the ladies to put it on the market. "People in England would be happy to buy great quantities." Flowers, wilting in the hot noon sun, were presented to her in a handle basket by Teacher's little daughter, and she expressed her gratitude for their generous hospitality and warm welcome, at the same time delicately dabbing her perspiring forehead with a pale blue embroidered handkerchief. When she left, the ladies beamed with satisfaction and wonder, marvelling that she had spent all of ten minutes with them.

"And what a nice refined lady she is, eh," Aunt Julia said, "such a charming and mannersable somebody, but is so white people stay."

In the yard at Mr. Simpson's, a coconut booth had been erected, decorated with croton, fern and asparagus vines with the coconut bow archway over the entrance, beautifully plaited by Mr. Bobsingh, the expert booth maker, whom everybody called Baboo. The Governor sipped his lemonade while his Lady drank freshly squeezed orange juice and then asked for coconut water. Mr. Rob had supplied ice (a rare commodity which he had carefully saved from the block he got last Friday)for the occasion. Mr. Simpson dressed in his top hat and long scissors tail coat, Miss Bell in her broad flowers-hat, as well as other chosen people dressed in their finery of various vintages and origins, were introduced to the Governor and his party, and when the story came out that the big red skin Police Inspector was Mr. Simpson's cousin, the old man could not hide his pride. "He is the son of my mother's second cousin on her father's side," he announced to the Governor. "Interesting, interesting," the Governor said. The visit ended with the Governor thanking them all, wishing them the best of luck as he waved goodbye and in a moment the motorcade was out of sight, on its way to the next town.

As soon as the motorcade was out of sight, the idle boys on the road side – a set of "camaroun, even-up" – who were not allowed to enter the yard during the visit, now turned their attention on Mr. Simpson.

"Bwoy, Mr. Simpson, you face boasy today though ee!"

"What you mean by that," he answered.

"Well, look how Governor come a you yard, me never know you was such a big shot," Percy said.

"Yes, Mr. Simpson, you highly man, the white Governor and his wife drink out a you glass eena you yard." That was Copey, Mr. Coley overgrown boy.

Percy continued, "Bwoy, Mr. Simpson, me have fi look on you different, imagine Governor come to you yard and big big Police Inspector a you cousin".

Mr. Simpson, enjoying the moment, pulled himself up to his full five feet two inches, his head bobbing from side to side, "All of unno teck people simple, just because I don't go around boasting and bragging about my relations, unno tink I ordinary, but just all of you remember, many a mawga cow you see a pasture, a bull muma."

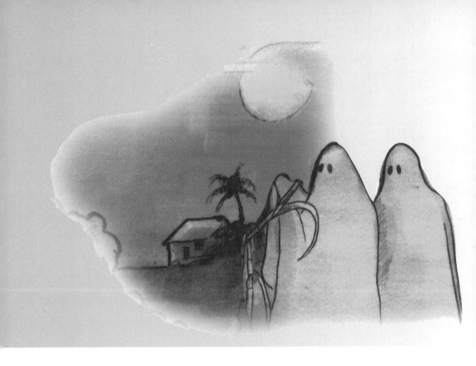

Deadlef

"**Y**ou ever si anyting like deadlef to cause enmity an strife among family, trouble top a trouble." Miss Conse was in distress when she heard the news that Mass John's children, same mother same father, were fighting over the legacy. He had married Miss Elvira when they were both young. Now the two old people died within a year of each other, first the mother and then the father. Both were buried a year apart, side by side on the day before Christmas Eve.

They had been married for over sixty years and lived a good, honest and productive life. They were not wealthy but as Miss Conse described them, "Them was God bless people". They owned their substantial house on eleven acres of roadside land on the main road, twenty-seven acres of beautiful land on the same road. Forty acres suitable for

farming or building in a fast developing district nearby. They also owned the three bedroom house they rented to Corporal and the adjoining shop, also rented to a good tenant. Added to that, there were several heads of valuable cows, goats and pigs on the property. There were the mules, the donkeys and the drays the old man hired out. All in all, substantial value. They had worked hard and achieved much. There was also quite a tidy sum in the bank and Credit Union. They were proudly independent, honourable people.

"But see here mam, as Mass John eyes close, dem don't even bury im good yet, dem don't even have the tomb building fi dem parents yet and di war start." Miss Conse was clearly disturbed. "You mean dat dem can't come together and work out dem business? I hope dem don't bother interefere wid Miss Gladys who teck care of the old people all dese years." Well, the war she referred to was the dispute between the four children – each of them now grown up, mature adults – over who should inherit what.

It seemed as if the old people made no will, no doubt relying on them to settle the property between them. But it was not happening. "Before dem get together dem a fight, Govament soon teck way everything, and it woulda serve dem right." Miss Conse was talking with Mass John's brother, Maas Butty who was so disgusted with the whole affair he refused to have anything to do with it.

"Maybe if you call dem together Maas Butty, dem might listen to yu."

"My dear Miss Conse yu think so, yu really think dem wi listen? I never know I would live to see the day when John pickney dem can't even agree. And the sad ting is dat dem is no pickney, dem is all big somebody. Lawyer will soon eat out dem money."

But really when you think about it, it was not all of them that was in the war. Miss Gladys, the oldest, the one who remained home and looked after the old people to the last, was not making a fuss. She was quite contented with her life. She had been living with her parents in the old family home all this while and the place was looking prosperous. Under her supervision the place was well cultivated and fruitful. With her little pension and what the others sent to their parents now and then, she managed. When she felt like it she had a few students for extra lessons paying a small fee. By all accounts the war over the estate did not really include her. Somehow, the others recognized what she had done for their parents, what they didn't do, so they left her alone and the property she lived on.

As Miss Conse observed, "At least they have the decency to acknowledge that."

The youngest son, Lenford, who was on scholarship abroad did not seem interested. His only comment was, "Whatever you others decide is ok." He was almost finished with the studies he had gone to pursue and soon he would have the promised promotion if he decided to return to his old job in the Government Service. That, however, did not seem likely as he had many good offers abroad and he had married a lady he had met in one of his classes. The report was that she was well established in her profession, owned her own home and was well set.

The real war was between Stanford and Ina, the sister before him. They were both working people, in good jobs, but they were just plain greedy. Each seemed to want everything. It didn't seem to matter that there was enough to go round. But these two had plans and were determined to get their own way. When their uncle called them together to see how the matter could be resolved, Gladys agreed.

Lenford said he would come down for a week to meet with them all. As was expected, Ina and Stanford did not agree, in fact it was a good two years before they agreed to meet.

By this time, Ina had put it in the hands of her lawyer, who advised her to meet with her siblings and settle. "If you all can do it out of court, all the better, simpler and less costly. If you want, I will act as mediator and give you whatever advice you need." Stanford objected to that He said, "Not one damn". As her lawyer, he thought he was bound to favour her in whatever discussion. There were, he said, several grandchildren to be considered. Gladys' son who wanted to be a doctor, and his three sons who wanted to be an architect, a chemist and an engineer. Ina said he brought up grandchildren because of the six, he had three. So in fact he would benefit more.

So the disagreement went on and on till Stanford threatened to abandon the whole idea of a meeting and go to court. He went as far as to say, it was reported, that if they persisted in their unfair ways he would do them bodily harm. That was one rumour, another was that he was on hard drugs. Happily, that turned out to be malicious talk. When Gladys invited the two grand-daughters to come and pick out pieces of crockery, cutlery, crochet, and to share the few pieces of jewelry and other things their grandmother had left, Stanford and Ina were not pleased. Ina wanted some of the real cotton sheets and pieces of crochet. For peace sake, Gladys allowed her to take them.

Ina was furious when she heard that Gladys had given the crochet tablecloth to Lenford's new wife. Their mother had gotten it as a wedding present and had preserved it all these years, using it only on rare and special occasions. It was a real heirloom. So Stanford felt it should go to his wife as he was the elder son. He sent his sister a message to say that nothing more should be given away until the court heard the case. The bitterness swept back and forth with every manner of insults and hurtful words.

To make matters worse, the two teenaged children of Stanford and Ina got into the quarrel. And these once close cousins stopped speaking to each other on the instruction and example of their warring parents.

"What a shame an disgrace een Miss Fan, look how those children was lovin, and di parents to. Look what dedlef doing to them, and you know is only things." Miss Conse was so upset, she had to vent her feelings to her best friend.

When Lenford heard what was happening, he called long distance from abroad, and gave them a piece of his mind. He advised them both to agree to the meeting, to sit down together like civilized people and settle the business. He threatened to further complicate the matter so none of them would live to benefit. He advised them to heed the advice of the lawyer and settle out of court, the only sensible thing to do, and save the embarrassment and exposure of a lawsuit that could take years. He had discussed it with a lawyer and a counsellor and a Priest, and they all gave that advice.

He informed them that he was arriving in two weeks time and he expected them to come to their senses and come to the meeting which he was arranging at the family home with Gladys. He ended by saying that that would be what their parents would expect and they should not, in fact could not, let them down.

At first Ina refused. "Who does he think he is to dictate to me." But her husband advised her that it was the best thing to do, and when she heard from her lawyer how long it would take to go through the litigation and the enormous

cost, she reluctantly changed her mind and agreed to the meeting.

Stanford, too, agreed when his son who was at college advised him and the meeting took place according to plan. They asked their uncle and a lawyer to sit with them. It was a good thing they did, for no sooner than they came together, the enmity and the name calling and the bitterness started, and you can guess who was responsible. This forced their uncle to remind them that they were blood relatives, same mother same father, and that what was happening was not acceptable. They should consider their children and the kind of example they were setting. It was bad, he said, and they should stop it. He made them promise that as a start, at that meeting they would be at peace and stop the name calling and the bitterness and for their own good and benefit, settle the matter peacefully. He ended by reminding them that if people of one set of parents could not do this in a decent and civil and peaceful manner then the world was doomed. He then made a list of all the property, starting with the money in the credit union and the bank. Both Stanford and Gladys together could access these amounts with no trouble as they were signatories to the accounts. Matter of fact, Gladys for the last four years or so, was the one who operated the accounts on behalf of her parents.

Their uncle, advised by the lawyer, was able to get them all to agree on a very reasonable and mutual settlement. Gladys would get the house and the land it was on and half of the money in the Credit Union. Stanford would get the acreage he said he wanted to rear cows. Ina would get the 27 acres of roadside land. Lenford would get the three bedroom house that was rented and the other half of the money in the Credit Union. The money in the bank would be used to pay all the little debts and the immediate expenses. The rest of the property would be sold to pay the lawyer and Government expenses for transfers and taxes. Whatever was left would be divided equally between the six grandchildren and the church of which the old people were members for ever so long.

It took only two hours to reach the agreement and their uncle was surprised. "Look how you all settle things so peaceful and nice. Unno shoulda did do this two years ago, but thank God it happen." He even got them to agree that they would consider putting something towards building the shopping centre that Ina was thinking of. "It would be a nice thing to honour the memory of yu Parents."

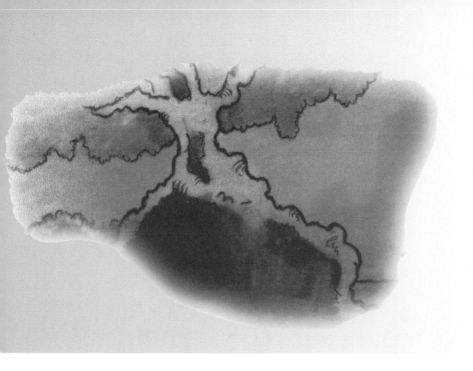

Godmother

In the village of Pleasant Valley near the border of three parishes, the Parkin family was well known to be a "haughty" set of people, some people would tell you that they were all "faasty" in a good sort of way. Every one of them, male and female alike, did not put up with nonsense and no one would dare take any steps with them, and if you happened to cross them, woe betide. They were what you would call "salt of the earth" Jamaican people with an independent pedigree from way back. They did not fail to "tell it like it is" when the occasions arose.

You can well imagine with that kind of background there were many disagreements and occasional differences between the formidable members of that family, as each had their own opinion on matters large and small and they could always be heard bickering and fussing among themselves. It never seemed to stop. Those on the outside looking on would think they disliked each other, for even at the church door sometimes you could hear them arguing. But that was among themselves. If anyone was foolish enough to cross any single one of them, the whole family would immediately gang up, close ranks on the offender who would have the more than a dozen family members to contend with, individually and collectively, and that was not something you would wish on your worst enemy. Many a story was told of the total devastation of those brave or foolish enough to be caught in that position.

So, then, it was no surprise what happened to Mrs. Rennie's daughter, the married one in Kingston. When she had her first child, a boy, she said she wanted the baby to be christened in the church in Pleasant Valley that her family had attended for generations. So her mother who was head cook and bottle washer in the church made the arrangements.

Among the arrangements, godparents had to be found. So Mrs. Rennie asked Miss Jessica the spinster matriarch of the Parkin family to be one. Now if the members of the Parkin family were haughty and proud, there was none moreso than Miss Jess. She was formidable, was known for her kindness and generosity and for her sharp and incisive tongue. She didn't let anyone forget that she was Miss Jessica Annabella Parkin JP, the oldest child of Charles Josephus Parkin JP and his wife Irene Nennita JP, who was the daughter of Mrs. Katrina Letitia Farquhrson JP, from whom the family was reported to have inherited much wealth. In addition, she Miss Jess was a college trained teacher, now retired. She was even, with some truth, said to be very wealthy, a very well respected lady and to a certain extent well feared. She was a pillar and benefactor of the church which, as she often reminded everyone, was built by her great great grandparents of blessed memory who were buried in the special family section in the church yard, and which church her family helped to maintain over the years.

So when her friend Mrs. Rennie asked her to be her grandchild's godmother, she readily agreed, but not before she reminded her that being a godparent was no simple matter and, unlike a lot of people that she knew, she took that responsibility seriously. Mrs. Rennie agreed. She wouldn't dare disagree, and when she told Miss Conse what Miss Jess had said she too agreed, "After all shi mus know she is a eddicated lady."

"True mam true," Mrs. Rennie said.

But that was the grandmother. Her daughter, the baby's mother, had ideas that were different. To her, godparents were a necessary nuisance and no more, and the Christening was a mere formality to be gotten out of the way so that evil spirits would not interfere with the child. They were just to be at the Christening to hold the baby and answer the questions the Parson asked. Never mind that the questions had them pledge to nurture the child in the faith. Miss Jess knew that the day of the Christening, and she reminded everyone that the correct way to describe the event was Baptism, not Christening, and that Baptism was the beginning of a personal relationship with Christ that was a lifelong association and that godparents and parents had the responsibility to help the child as it grows to maintain that relationship.

When some of her acquaintances of other churches disagreed with infant Baptism, Miss Jess was heard to strongly defend her church's position on the matter, "Just as how parents make all the decisions for their children from birth, feed, clothes, school, those ordinary everyday matters, how much more it is their right and bounden duty to choose the Christian way of life for them. When they grow up and have sense they are to be guided to affirm that faith in Confirmation to which godparents are to help to nurture them."

She always ended with, "Any day you stop choosing feed and all the other things for your infant children, I will stop support baptising infants.

"Amen Miss Jess ... Amen," Miss Conse agreed.

So here was the godmother with differing if not opposing views from the baby's mother, widely mistaken ideas. Even so, when the second child, a girl, came, Miss Jess was again asked to stand for her as well. And so she did.

Things went relatively smoothly over the years and since they resided all the way in Kingston, Miss Jess could only enquire, and so she had information only periodically. When they were ten years old Miss Jess gave Mrs. Rennie a ewe kid for each of them. The goats proved to be very fertile and before long each child had a tidy little bank account from their increase. Miss Jess was very pleased and when she heard that they were now attending good Church Schools, she sent them "a little something for books". Now that they were of the age to consider confirmation, she made it known that it was quite time. When they began to go to instructions she was happy and tried to keep in touch with them.

One Christmas when they came home to spend the holidays with their grandparents, they paid their godmother a visit, the first in a long while. The visit did not go well, because Miss Jess was not pleased with their manners and appearance. She expected them not only to be polite and

pleasant, but more respectful and "mannersable". She did not have much experience with teenagers from the big city. Though they were not disrespectful, they were far from the humble and meek children she expected. For example, they answered "yes" and "no" as necessary, not the "Yes Goddy Jess" or "No Goddy Jess" as was customary for country children to say, and as she expected them to. To top it all, the young lady had arrived at her godmother's house in a scanty rib tickler and a short shorts, the in thing for teenagers. The young man had on a sleeveless T shirt out of his pants, sorry out of his tight knee-length bike shorts. Miss Conse, when she saw them on the road, also disapproved with the remark "Is what dem young people coming to."

Miss Jess was quite shocked and said so. She roundly chastised them with her sharp tongue and advised them that they were not to go on the street in that kind of garb. She couldn't call them clothes. She also had a word for their grandmother whom she said should be ashamed to walk with them like that on the public road. During the ensuing conversation when in answer to her query she discovered that they had both decided not to get confirmed in the coming Easter, she had a fit.

After she had Mrs. Rennie properly told she spoke to their mother. She made it known that she did not approve of the way they spoke and the way they dressed, and more than all the loose way they seemed to be growing up. No wonder, she said, for their parents set no good example for them as they themselves were living an ungodly life.

They did not attend church and only now and then sent the children; that kind of lifestyle was clearly responsible for their poor behaviour and their decision not to be confirmed. Needless to say, the children's mother was very hurt by her remarks and, as she herself was a very formidable lady, she made Miss Jess know how she felt. The clash of these two ladies and their conversation did not end well, in fact it ended quite badly, as she told Miss Jess, "It is really none of your business how I grow my children", that she was downright rude and interfering and she best leave her business alone. In shock, Miss Jess reminded her it was her God given duty and obligation which she had pledged to God to honour.

"And after all it was your mother who asked me to stand for the children."

"Well it was not me, it was my mother, I did not ask you."

That last remark cut Miss Jess very deeply. "God be with you my dear," were her parting words.

Miss Conse was livid. "What an ungrateful woman, no mannas, Kingston spwile har Miss Vie, is so dem gwan."

When Mrs. Rennie heard about the encounter, she was most apologetic. She was very sorry, she said, for she valued Miss Jess's friendship and support.

"Forgive the girl you hear Miss Jess," she pleaded, but she was preaching to the converted.

"My dear Miss Rennie, I forgive her as I hope to be forgiven, and I pray daily for them all."

But as the years passed, there was understandably a certain amount of tension and strained feelings between them. They remained friends but not as close as before. When they spoke, it was quite cordial and polite but lacking the customary warmth they had always shared.

Year after year, there were no more visits from the young people, no contact. But according to the story they later shared, they never stopped praying for each other and about the situation. "Every day and every night I take it to the foot of the cross," Mrs. Rennie told her friends and Miss Conse encouraged her, "Dats all yu can do mam, leave it to God."

A few years later, it was Christmas again. Miss Jess was sitting on her verandah a few days before, in fact the Saturday before Tuesday the real day. Who should she see coming up the pathway but Mrs. Rennie, her daughter and her two grandchildren, now handsome, modest young people.

Mrs. Rennie called out, "Hold dog, hold dog."

Miss Jess called out to the yard boy, "Leon, put up the dogs, visitors coming."

When she was sure they were secure she called to the visitors, "Come, come." They came safely up to the verandah, said their good evenings politely, and Miss Jess answered courteously.

It was Mrs. Rennie's daughter who first spoke, "Miss Jess, things have not been too good between us."

"Well it was none of my doing."

"I realize that I am to blame, that's why we have decided to come to you today to say how sorry we are and to apologize and ask your forgiveness."

She was struck by the sincerity in the young woman's voice, and after a brief pause Miss Jess said, "Well I am glad to see you have come to your senses and do the right thing. Of course I forgive you, I did so from the very day we had that unfortunate exchange of words, for I am a God fearing woman, and maybe I myself was a little too harsh with you."

The visit ended with Mrs. Rennie informing Miss Jess that, come Easter, the two children would be duly confirmed, and they expected her to be there. Their father would come to fetch Mrs. Rennie for the occasion and they had reserved space in the vehicle for her. When she hesitated, the children both said, "Goddy, you must come." Miss Jess was pleased no end, and for the very first time in their long friendship, Mrs. Rennie was sure that she saw Miss Jess wipe away a drop of eyewater. Her voice nearly broke as she said, "All I can say is that God answers prayer, for I have never stopped praying for them and for this day. The Lord be praised."

As planned, godmother Jess was in Kingston to witness the confirmation of her two godchildren, and from that day she was close to them, and they to her, until the day she died at the ripe old age of ninety. It was a sad time for them all. They were there for her burial and her godson, now a university student, read one of the lessons. He read so beautifully and was complimented by many persons for his splendid reading. As one lady remarked, "You read so intelligently and with such feeling, you know you would make a good Parson." That remark found room in his thoughts and heart.

Months later he received word from a lawyer, informing him that in her will Miss Jess had provided for him and his sister, quite handsomely, money for their university education. They went by appointment to see him. The lawyer said, "With that kind of money you both can attend any university in the world you choose. I hope you make the best use of this. Not many people have that opportunity." When he returned home, his thoughts were on his godmother and he wished that he had been closer to her. That same day he made a call to the Theological College.

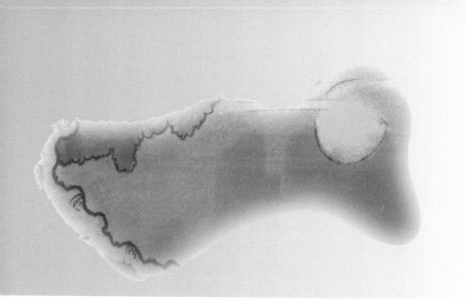

Fallen Angel and the Old Firestick

The scandal rocked the little village as the news went round with such speed that it wasn't long, a matter of days, before the whole district, everyone, was talking about this totally unexpected happening, this devastating news.

Brother Gray's wife of over thirty years "leave im and gone" after she administered a good thrashing to him as well as the person whom she said had caused the whole miserable affair.

It was the most unlikely and surprising of events. Brother Gray was the respected leader of the church at Charley's Run, well liked if not loved by everyone as a good Christian leader and preacher whose blood-and-fire sermons stirred the hearts of young and old alike. His church had a steady membership of some four hundred souls who came from as far away as Twelve-Miles and even beyond to his little church for the healing services and regular worship on Sundays and some week days.

Twice, he had to extend the little building, some say with his wife's money. She was a very successful higgler who traded the market in the nearest large town, and she was a buyer and seller of livestock, making quite a handsome profit. She was very involved in and supportive of her husband in his church work, sometimes quite aggressively, to the point where people felt she was the real leader. For instance, without his knowledge she had discussed with the elders the building of a baptism pool in the churchyard so they wouldn't have to walk the almost two miles to the river bridge twice a year for baptism. No wonder she found the journey taxing: she weighed over two hundred pounds and she felt the ceremonies couldn't take place without her. Needless to say when she told him of the plan, as he always did, Brother Gray agreed with her and his only remark was, "Is true mi dear wi need the pool," and once againing the formidable lady got what she wanted. He was totally submissive to her in most matters to do with the running of their life. Maybe because he was so committed and engrossed in the preaching and leading his flock that the everyday things were left to his wife, but this did not go unnoticed as Miss Conse often remarked, "Ah she wear the trousis you know...a she rule."

His congregation loved and revered him none the less even as he loved and cared for them. They all belonged to him. They were his flock, his sheep his children. To quote Miss Conse, "Yu couldn't want a better pastor." But he didn't put up with any foolishness. He was uncompromising on the matter of sin among his people, particularly the sins of the flesh. Many and long were the

sermons he preached against immorality, fornication, adultery, lasciviousness and lechery. Many were the young and not so young men and women he would "read out" of the membership if they were found out or sometimes even suspected of being in breach of the strict codes he set them. Those sins, he said would, surely drive you down to hell fire and damnation. His sermons on these matters would end with the warning, "Brothers and sisters beware, take heed that you do not fall into those sins, pray daily that the Lord will lead you far away from that path of certain destruction."

Needless to say, that kind of preaching drove the fear of the Almighty into the hearts of his hearers and in that fear and trembling the Amens were many, loud and strong, "Amen, Amen." "Preach the word brother", " Preach it pastor". No doubt, Brother was a powerful preacher especially when he was on what appeared his favourite topic. Said Miss Conse, "You ever si how im love preach about the sins of the flesh? and for him dat mean only one thing, man an woman business."

Oh yes, Brother was no ordinary preacher. His fame spread far and wide. Ever since he took over the church from its founder, a good friend and colleague of many years now ageing, he and by Miss Loona his wife, put their stamp on the growing congregation and their reputation spread, and he became well known specially for his preaching.

His was an interesting story. He and his close friend and colleague were converted the same night at a crusade meeting held by some visiting missionaries from abroad. They joined up with the new movement but after about a year they discovered that the visitors were not sincere. Matter of fact they found out that they were a bunch of racketeers who were collecting what amounted to large sums of money from unsuspecting poor persons all to assure them a place in the Kingdom. They barely escaped being arrested. The Police were just about to close in on them when, as was their true form, they disappeared from the island leaving the congregation without a leader.

So quite disillusioned and broken hearted, his older friend decided to form his own church and invited his young friend to join him. The other members of the now abandoned church were invited and quickly there was a growing membership and they soon moved into their own building in the heart of the capital city. Over the years, as Brother Gray matured in the church, he became well known. He married Miss Loona who was also a member.

Brother Gray was the chief lieutenant of the founder, and when it was decided to set up a church in Charley's Run, the founder's birthplace, and their first to be established in the rural areas, Brother Gray was the person chosen to lead that church. It was not long before five other branch churches were set up and, apart from running his own, Brother Gray assisted the aging founder in the supervision of the other churches, so quite often he had to be away from home. But Miss Loona would carry on while he was gone. She loved that, as it gave her a sense of power. At times Sister Clarice, the chief Sunday School teacher, would accompany Brother Gray on his trips, to assist him in training the newly recruited teachers.

In a little while Brother Gray was to become the powerful Pastor that he was, a man of God committed to his calling and regarded as the logical person to take over the reins as head of the church.

So now you can image what a shock and horror the whole district experienced, and the other branches as well, when the story spread that Brother Gray was seen hugging up and rubbing down Sister Clarice, and of all places in front

of the altar table in the Church. Like everybody else, Miss Conse was in shock, "Whey yu a say mah, Brother Grey? Mi can believe it. Man a dawg doh enn?"

"True wud, yu caan trus none a dem," agreed Miss Vie.

There were many who believed the story, including Miss Loona. All the try Brother Gray tried to explain she wouldn't even listen. She knew he was guilty as hell. He tried to tell her. Yes, he was hugging her but it was not for the reason they all believed. But wives know more than husbands think they know, his wife said. She had seen the signs, so she said. He explained that he had come into the church to see Sister Clarice kneeling at the penitential rail, praying and sobbing. He knelt beside her and put his arm around her shoulder to support and comfort her as he had done to many others, man and woman, in similar circumstances. She began to tell him that she just had news that her younger brother had murdered his girlfriend and their little baby girl and then killed himself, and as she didn't want anybody to hear the horrible story she spoke in Spanish which he also spoke. To further comfort and talk to her he took her into the vestry so she could talk freely in private.

That was his story. But what he couldn't explain was the brassiere that it was said the cleaner found in the vestry the same day and which she promptly took to Miss Loona. Putting two and two together, the hugging, the trips together, the brassiere, the Spanish speaking, Miss Loona was sure something was into something and no one could convince her otherwise. She had always suspected them, she said, and spread the word about their affair.

Armed with the latest piece of evidence, Miss Loona went straight to Sister Clarice's house. Now these two women were the opposite of each other, both in stature and behaviour. One slim and frail, one big and powerful, loud and aggressive, the other very prim and proper.

"Listen Sister man teif. You think I don't know what going awn between yu and mi husband inna di church... Unno is a damn disgrace."

Confronted by her attacker, Sister Clarice was as high toned as could be. "I have no idea what you are taking about. Just you leave my home with your vulgar display at once."

"Leave yu yard, not before I get my satisfaction...come meck a show yu vulgar display yu likkle maaga adulterer."

With that, she grabbed her and gave Sister Clarice such a thrashing in full view of everyone who had quickly gathered to witness the incident. Poor Sister Clarice was no match for the heavyweight. It took three strong men to pull the two hundred pounder from the bantam weight when it was clear to the bystanders that Miss Loona would have beaten her to death. By the next day the song was out "Bantam caant mach heavy weight, Oh dat is murder, sure murder." An she couldn even bawl," said Miss Conse as she relayed the news of the beating.

But that was not the end of the matter as the bystanders thought. Miss Loona then moved next to the church where she pulled a surprised Brother Gray from the Bible study he was conducting for some young people and gave him his ample share of the beating. She collared him and sent him sprawling with one swing of her head to his forehead butting him to the ground. "Lawd she throw Katie pon him", laughed the idle boys watching and as he fell she jumped astride his chest and proceeded to pulverize his face with her fists ,yelling her accusations in punctuation of the blows.

"Yu disgraceful hippocrite brute yu...and call yuself preacher, God gwine strike yu dung. Fornicator... adulterer... lecherer.".

Mercifully he was out like a light so he hardly felt those blows. In all this, he offered no resistance like a lamb to the slaughter. Again, it took some strong men to pull her off the bruised and battered preacher and hold her long enough for others to help him up to escape further fury, but not before his enraged wife had her say.

Pulling herself to her nearly six feet height, straightening her clothes, she yelled to her disgraced husband, "Yu Lucky dem man hold mi...I am taking the evening train to my sister in Montego Bay...Today is Wednesday...Ah coming back next week Monday morning bright an early an don't meck a si yu when ah come back. Get yuself outa mi house and don't ever meck a si yu ugly face again as long as ah live... Judas. "

With that, she spat at him and was off. It wasn't long however that everybody realized that that was perhaps the excuse the ambitious and envious evil lady was looking for to take over the church which she wanted for herself. She long coveted it and tolerated her husband as he was the better preacher and drew the crowds to them. Now she had it, for the very next day Brother Gray took the mail car to Santa Cruz to his brother. Sister Clarice, to the jeers and taunts of the cruel villagers, a day later was on the train to Kingston with her two brown grips. Then the song came out, "Brother gone, an Sister gone, one to east an one to west, gone to a far far home forever with satan and leave the pugilist to rule the flock she one, amen amen so let it be".

True to her ambitions, Miss Loona took over the church, which strangely enough grew and prospered even beyond her own expectations. She gave up the higglering and became known as the caring pastor who fed and clothed the poor and the sick, from the tithes her people brought in. All this improvement she was sure was the Lord's doing for she had banished the devils from among their midst. Her favourite topic when she preached was "giving".

"The Lord said give me what is mine and I will bless and prosper you in a way you cannot begin to imagine."

So the people gave, so their church prospered. She fell out with the head church because she would take no advice from them, broke off from them, became affiliated to a denomination in America, changed the name and she was made a Bishop. Soon after her installation ceremony she bought a brand new Chevrolet car. Money had begun to come in from the Americans and she could not be happier.

By now she was so popular and powerful that it all seemed to go to her head. She started to preach against all other churches, such as the Anglicans up the road who had the school. She told her people that the children were being taught the wrong doctrine that Jesus was God come to earth. She preached about the "Graven images" being worshipped by the Roman Catholics who had a crucifix above their altar; about the Seventh day Adventists who didn't work on Saturdays; about the Salvation Army for – according to her – collecting for the poor only at Christmas time; against the Baptists, Methodists, Moravians. No other denomination escaped her bitter tongue. She went to a place in Kingston, so she said, to improve her English and speech, necessary, she said, as she was now a Bishop. She fixed up her house, wore the most elaborate robes when she didn't wear the most spectacular hats to match her costly dresses. She felt she could do anything, and you couldn't stop Miss Loona, she was a law unto herself and people began to be afraid of her. Some people disliked her. Miss Conse for instance, "Mi no go near her yu know ma, ef you no go a fowl roos, im wont filth pon yu head."

All this time, no one heard a word from Brother Gray, or about him, nor Sister Clarice. Once Miss Loona tried to find her estranged husband to have him sign over the ownership of the property, which they jointly owned, to make her sole owner, but he could not be found, so that matter remained unresolved as was her marriage to Brother Gray as she did not believe in divorce and he never showed his face in that village ever since that fateful day years ago.

All was going well till one day near Christmas Miss Loona was preaching to a packed church, and she was in her element, prancing and shouting as usual, but this day a little more than usual. She seemed possessed. She now weighed over three hundred pounds and the doctor had told her to lose weight, which advice she ignored. She was up and down as vigorously as ever, causing people to marvel at her agility. So they were not prepared for what happened that December day. Miss Loona, or rather Bishop Loona, collapsed in the middle of the preaching and fell on the hard concrete floor. Before the brethren could reach her and render assistance, she made one last gasp, her eyes rolled over to show the bare white and Bishop Loona Gray of the American Church of God's True Saints in Charley's Run was dead. The doctor who performed the post mortem said it was a massive heart attack. No wonder, he said, she was grossly overweight. "But she look so strapping and strong" was the comment of many of the flock. Miss Conse was not so kind, "She nyam too much, mi hear say she like pork fat an eat as much as two poun a corn pork at a time. She too craven."

The funeral which took place some ten days later was the largest the village had ever seen, with people coming from all over the island as well as many from abroad. They came in trucks, buses, cars vans and by train. The expanded church building was not nearly big enough to hold the people, and there were three times as many outside as could hold inside. Elder Parkins from a neighbouring church was there assisting the American Bishop who barely arrived in time for the service. All went well as could be expected. There were six tributes, two remembrances and a eulogy, two solos and renditions by the choir. When all of this was done, three hours later, Elder asked if there was anyone else who wanted to speak.

To everyone's surprise, who should step through the crowded doorway and up the aisle having alighted from a fancy motor car that had just pulled up but Brother Gray, looking a little older, strong, as sharp and prosperous as ever in his well fitted suit of black serge a striped shirt and a neat well matched tie of silk brocade. Right behind him was Sister Clarice "dressed to puss back foot", looking so elegant and sharp in a nice suit and a pretty hat. There was a murmur as Brother Gray stepped up, growing louder almost to applause as Sister Clarice walked in behind him and took a seat behind the family bench. You couldn't miss her dark purple suit, fussy hat, and long gloves all befitting her success and her new station in life. As she was passing a group of women one whispered, "Sister Clarice, a you dat?"

"Yes my dear, me same one, I wouldn't miss this funeral for anything in the world.". Miss Conse remarked, "An she brazen fi true. Puss bruck cokenat in her her eye."

Brother Gray was allowed to speak. In his short sermon he called the congregation to repentance and forgiveness, "Because you know not the hour nor the day when it will be your call."

Brother Gray then announced that he and Sister Clarice would be married shortly. They were now both ordained Ministers and had pastored quite a prosperous church in a neighbouring island. However, they would be taking over the church now that Bishop had been called to higher service and they would shortly be returning to his beloved flock which he was forced to leave. He wasn't quite sure if the enthusiastic Amen was in reference to that announcement or in reference to the Bishop being called to higher service.

Later he was able to explain that up to the dreadful day years ago he and Sister Clarice had not been romantically involved and were totally innocent of the charges that were made by his scheming wife and that the brassiere which figured as evidence was planted as part of the plot to get rid of him. This the cleaner who allegedly found the article later verified. He had decided to go back to Bible school unknown to Sister Clarice; as God would have it unknown to him, she also decided to go to the same school. They met again, became good friends and the memory of the incident only served to bring them closer together. After ordination they worked apart for some time, and then together for two years during which time they knew they wanted to be together for life. He was just about to file for his divorce, when they got the news of Miss Loona's death. Her passing was a blessing in disguise as he was now free, and the sole owner of the property in Charley's Run.

The whole affair was the talk of the village for years. Many felt it was how the Lord intended things to be. There were those who didn't like the return of the former "fallen" Pastor, others rejoiced at the news of his innocence and his imminent return. Still others couldn't care less. As for Brother Gray and Sister Clarice, they had long since forgiven Miss Loona and often prayed for her. They got married and proceeded with the Lord's work.

As Sister Plunkett, Goddy B and some other women including Miss Conse met one day over the corn shelling and talked of the matter, they were, they said, amazed at how the Lord worked out things in good time. The church had fallen right back into Brother Gray's hands where it rightfully belonged, in their opinion. It was a Miracle. Miss Conse had the right comment, "What is fi yu, cannot be un fi yu" and Goddy B added "An what is not fi you can never be fi yu," at which they all had a hearty laugh and got on with their shelling.

Church and Me

At a time and a place
When I could barely speak
Granny hauled me to church
Pushed and shoved me there
Every first day of the week.
I had no choice then
I dared not protest
What good would it do
God was there she said
"Child it was all for the best."

So it became a real habit
Though reluctantly I went
Religiously every Sunday bell
And friends were there too
Some taken some sent.
There I learnt much
Had a great deal of fun
Heard of God's mercy
His goodness and love
So now I am glad I had gone.

For when Sunday comes
Wherever I am I gladly go
Not as a child unwillingly
But as a grown man eagerly
To His house where I met him long ago.
My son now is quite regular
For I did not spare the rod
He says he is grateful
For in his own youth
He has found the same God.

Morning After

First bell had just started to ring that Sunday morning in June and Aunt Clarice for the first time in living memory was late for church. Most Sunday mornings by then she had reached as far as Miss Wilson's gate with only a couple chains to go to reach the old cut stone church on the level common right in the middle, between the two sugar estates. Every Sunday since she was a young lady and had married the shoe maker and come to live in the village she worshipped in that church sitting in the same seat, rain or shine, morning or evening, year in year out. Two years ago when he sickened and died she buried him in the churchyard and life went on.

This morning she was vexed with herself as she listened to the bell calling, according to the school children, "Come

sinner come, come sinner come". She was still struggling with the new brassiere that her niece had sent her last Christmas. Apart from the fact that it was a size too small, the June heat was causing her to perspire more than ever despite the nice cold bath she had earlier. For the last few minutes she was fighting the brassiere strap without success. She was in no mood for that kind of problem. She wanted to get to church early so she would have time before service start to share with her best friend Aunt Essie, the latest about Caleb and Doris, and all the trouble she was having with her nephew and the new woman he had taken up with. This woman was not even divorced from her second husband, and the news was that Corporal was looking for her to serve her the papers for bigamy, for she was still married according to law to her first husband. She got the news late yesterday afternoon and she was anxious to tell her friend, as much as she was anxious to get to church on time.

She was late that morning because the stupid boy Rennal who worked with her did not turn up for work, she surmised just because there was a little rain early, just before daybreak. The four goats had to be taken out to the grass piece nearby and she had to do it.

"Botheration!" she exclaimed as the elastic strap she was tugging at to catch the two hooks, slipped out of her fingers and snapped back.

"Get behind mi satan," she said as she caught hold of the strap again, and holding her breath to small up her chest she finally managed to get the strap to meet, fastened the two hooks, and with difficulty put the two number forties into the two thirty eight cups. She was convinced that it was the devil that had caused the difficulty, not the size of the garment.

That done, she turned her attention to the shoes, and was just about to put her two stockinged feet into her comfortable church shoes, when she heard the calling, "Aunt Clarice, Aunt Clarice oh."

"Ah who dat?" she called back moving to the front door.

"Me Annabelle." She opened the door to see her neighbour, young Belle, standing there in her tear up nightie, her mouth wide open, breathless.

"Wha happen Belle?" she asked the girl.

Before she could answer, Aunt Clarice shouted to Rennal who was just opening the little gate to come into the yard, "Rennal a now yu comin."

Belle caught her breath. "Lord Jeesas! Aunt Clarice, Lord."

"Wha happen gal, what happen?"

Belle kept moaning, "Lord, Lord mam."

Aunt Clarice guided her to the bench, "Come siddung an ketch yu breath, come. Rennal bring some water. Belle, wha happen?"

Belle managed to calm down just enough to haltingly say "Lord Jeesas, Mother P drop dung, an her eye dem turn over, she naw blow an it look like she ded."

"Lord have mercy, is what dis pon mi dis morning," Clarice said as she quickly pulled off her church dress and hauled on a loose house dress, pushed her feet into her yard shoes.

As she was going through the door she felt the pinch of the new brassiere. She quickly pulled the dress almost over her head, calling "Come Belle pull the brassiere strap." That done, she reached inside the dress and pulled the brassiere out, threw it on the sofa in the sitting hall and was through the door calling, "Rennal ketch up the fire and put on the peas, seet a soak in the blue enamel pot pon the kitchen

table, just put it awn the fire till a come back...Lord have mercy no church today."

She moved as quickly as her large frame would allow, down the path to Mother P's, almost slipping on the two flat stones at Fanny's gate. As she turned into the yard she saw Deacon Williams in his church clothes coming towards the house, "Morning Brother Will." As they exchanged greetings they were on the verandah, where the old lady was sitting in her large wooden chair, propped up with a pillow and a cushion, her grandson fanning her with her church fan. She herself was just about to leave for church, when she collapsed.

"Mother P, Mother P," Aunt Clarice called. No answer. Deacon called, "Miss Pigin, Miss Pigin," her name which was shortened to Mother P. Still no answer came, the old lady appeared quite lifeless. Through her half closed lids you could see the white portion of her eyes, the condition described as "Her eye dem turn over."

Gently but firmly Aunt Clarice slapped both her cheeks, "Mother P, Mother P, come open yu eye, first bell ring already, come ole lady come, church time."

That seemed to do the trick. The old lady moaned, moved her head to the side, patted her stomach and mumbled something they couldn't understand. Deacon took her hands and patted them, calling, "Mother P, Mother P." The only answer was a moan, the old lady pointing to her stomach. Aunt Clarice, now realizing that there was something wrong in that region, said to Belle, "Draw some ginger tea, hurrry up." She reached to her side pulling down the zip and put her hand down the dress back and freed the brassiere strap. Deacon advised, "meck it strong."

The morning's tea water was already on the fire, boiling vigorously, and in no time Belle brought the steaming cup of ginger tea. The fanning had continued and it was clear that the old lady was reviving. Aunt Clarice held the white enamel mug to her lips, "Come Mother P, teck time sip it, come mi darling, try."

She obliged and, with eyes still half closed, she began to drink the tea. After a few good gulps, almost halving the cup she rubbed her stomach, and holding on to two arms of the chair she braced herself and let out a great big belch, and simultaneously eased up and broke a wind that you could hear from out the road.

At the same time she opened her eyes, smiled and said, "Thank di Lord" and she was fine from that moment.

"Mother P, well sar yu frighten wi." It was Aunt Clarice, wiping the old lady's face with the rag Belle handed her.

Mother P looked up at her friends, "Tank unno yah, mi sorry fi di trouble but is dat damn peas soup ah eat fi dinner too late last night."

"You have to be careful," Deacon advised, "Wi glad yu recover," and he was on his way to church, all be it late.

Aunt Clarice didn't reach church that Sunday, the first time in years that this ever happened. She took great delight in telling the story of how she rescued mother P from the jaws of death, how the sounds the old lady made were like the two factory Korchie answering one another, and how she had to miss church that day because of Mother P's incident. She not only missed church, she didn't get a chance to tell her friend the hot news she had intended. All the better, for later that same Sunday, she found out that the news was false after all, the work of some malicious and envious person. The story she intended to tell was, as she described it, "Pure unadulterated lie an mischief. Ef mi did tell anybody dat news mi woulda inna di lie an story tu... Gawd move in mysterious ways." To which Deacon replied, "An sometime in a mischievous way his wonders to perform."

The Little Red Train

"My dear Miss Clar, the gal in the family way, and what is more she either don't know who it for, or she not telling anyone, not even her mother."

"Say what Miss Constance!" Miss Clar's mouth dropped open and Miss Constance covered it with the little handle basket she took to the shop and looked around to make sure no one else was hearing.

"Yes, my dear mam, you can imagine the poor mother she."

"Serve her right," Miss Clar said as Mrs Felix, Ruby's mother, was known to be the village snob and for that reason disliked by the other women.

It was really hard to believe the latest story that was going the rounds. Ruby Felix, the one and only daughter of

Mr. Paul and Mrs. Josephine Felix, church pillars and stalwarts in the district, the prettiest girl for miles around, was really pregnant, and by all accounts didn't know or wouldn't say who the baby father was. That was the new story circulating in the village and everywhere – church, shop, market, clinic, post office – everywhere you went that was the talk.

Ruby's mother, in an effort to hide her embarrassment, invented all kinds of stories, varying with each enquirer as to why Ruby, the leading soprano on the Church of England choir, was not in church for the past few weeks well. She was sick, she had the measles, she was studying for exams, or she was visiting her aunt in Kingston. That was after she was spirited by night out of the district by her father who had one of the three cars in the district. But those stories, even though they fooled many people, didn't fool Miss Constance who knew more about everybody's business than the people themselves.

"No mam, nothing no go so, she pregnant."

Well it seemed that things didn't go too well between the "aunt in Kingston" and Ruby because it was not long before she returned to the district with a bouncing baby boy and a wedding ring (bought by her mother) and everybody was told that her new name was Mistress Davis and that her husband worked on a ship that only came into Jamaica once a year. Needless to say there were those who believed the story about the seaman but the majority didn't. Certainly not Miss Constance, as she stated in no uncertain terms to Mother P last week Tuesday when she bucked up the old lady in the shop. "No mam, Mother P, take it from me as I tell you, is her own cousin Fonso do the damage. You ever see how the two a dem tick lika peas soup. Is no one but him."

This was one time when Miss Constance was half correct. Most of the time she was totally wrong even though she dished out her news as gospel. Fonso and Ruby were indeed thick. They were two sisters' children and they were close from infancy like brother and sister, loving and caring toward each other. He also was an only child, two years older than Ruby. As Fonso told Percy, Mr. Logan's son, when he tried to get fresh with Ruby, "listen bwoy, mi wi kill fi her you know."

Because of this closeness between the two cousins there was this feeling by some folks that they were lovers and it didn't help matters when Fonso fell down off the crane at the factory, and as he was unconscious for about half hour everyone thought he was dead. As Ruby got the news she fainted and Nurse had to rub her up with bay rum. It turned out that Fonso only had a broken wrist but in her distress Ruby had told her mother she didn't know what she would do if Fonso had died.

To make matters worse, Fonso was the one who went to wherever she went to have the baby and brought her home, and since then was like the baby's father, always around. Every evening as he came home from work, sometimes before he even went home, he was there. He couldn't be more attentive. Everyone knew this was so. Miss Constance concluded, "is only the baby father woulda behave in that manner."

The truth about the child's father was no great mystery but the family guarded the secret well. Ruby had gone to Mandeville to spend a week with her cousin and that is where she met the baby's father. He was her first lover. She got pregnant and he would have married her, according to him, only his parents were adamant that no marriage should take place because he was under-aged, eighteen to be exact, and she was perhaps too old (twenty one), but certainly too black! They were quite wealthy people, almost white, as Mother P would later, much later, say, "a threaten fi white".

He was shipped off to England to school and they thought the matter ended there. But he wrote her sometimes twice a week. The letters were sent to Fonso in Balaclava where he worked. As you can well imagaine, Ruby looked forward to the letters and read each one over and over again till the next arrived. The letters were like a love story book, as the young man poured out his heart, his longing for his love and his anxiety for her welfare and that of their child. He vowed as soon as he could he would come home to her and make things right.

Ruby would spend the days reading and savouring the lovely loving things he wrote and then when she had digested all, settled down to write to him. She gave him news about the baby, how he was doing. She had christened him "Michael Paul Lorenzo Davis". Lorenzo for his father and Michael Paul for his two grandfathers, and he was called "Larry".

Michael Paul Lorenzo was christened in the church she herself was christened in. But perhaps because the parson doubted the story of the marriage, Ruby was denied the thanksgiving prayers at the altar rail which were traditional for married mothers. Miss Josie was furious but Mr. Felix quieted her down. "Josie don't push you luck, no stir up no ants nest."

Ruby didn't mind. Her baby was christened. Her baby's father loved her and she lived for the day when he would return to Jamaica. She was sure he would marry her then. Miss Josie stuck to her story and Mr. Felix really didn't have much to say about the matter. He couldn't care less. Ruby was his only daughter and that was that. He didn't discuss it with anyone, not his brother, Rufus, nor his sister, Kate. Not even with his wife. He provided for them as best as he could, quite handsomely, for he was not a man of straw. He was enjoying his grandson and by the time the boy was two he taught him all the little things grandfathers taught their grandsons at that age. The latest thing he bought was a colt for the boy and on most afternoons he and the little boy tended the colt and talked about learning to ride when the time came, when the colt was ready.

Gradually the district gossip subsided about Ruby and the baby. Other new and more juicy stories now occupied their minds and tongues. The fact too that the baby was obviously "white man pickney" made even Miss Constance concede that it "really don't look like Fonso is the father after all, but as far as dat go, between Fonso and Ruby, something in a something."

Ruby ignored the talk and every evening she bathed and tidied her son and walked with him the four chains to the edge of her father's property in time to see the evening train come over the little hill and run by the length of the property line and disappear around the bend on the journey to Montego Bay. By now Larry was talking and had such a love for the trains that he would pull his mother towards the line even when it wasn't time for their walk, shouting, "train, train, whoo, whoo."

Ruby herself was twice as eager now, especially since the letter she got Friday. Lorenzo was coming home. She couldn't believe it. It wasn't time yet. He hadn't finished his studies – it would be another two years before he qualified – but he was homesick and he was missing her and wanted to see his son, growing to look more like his father every day, Ruby thought. Besides, he was now twenty-one and his parents couldn't stop him.

Ruby's mother and father also anxiously awaited the arrival of this mysterious young man. He should have come for Christmas six months ago, but something happened and he had disappointed Ruby and everybody. Her mother especially, as that was the second time they had had the disappointment. She was beginning to doubt if there really was a Lorenzo. His parents just refused to send him the money for his passage and he hadn't enough of his own, and then he was not allowed to work. But things had changed. He definitely was coming. And she and Fonso made plans to meet him. That would solve a lot of problems – at last the district and all those who had bad-mouthed her would see for themselves at last that her baby's father was real.

Today was Wednesday and by this time tomorrow he would be almost here. Had he changed? What did he look like now? She was sure his easy winning smile was the same as she remembered it to be. Other memories stirred now – of their first meeting, their first loving, the ecstatic weekend they had had at that time. The tearful parting and the desperation she felt then. She remembered too the promises he had made, repeated in each of his letters. She thought – one more day, one more day, and all her longing and her dreams would be fulfilled. He had said in his letter that he had bought a pretty train engine for their son. It was red and could run and whistle just like a real train. Larry would be so pleased – his own train. She could imagine him playing on the length of the paved verandah with his new train.

All that night she couldn't sleep. Larry too was excited in anticipation of his daddy's arrival. Finally he went to sleep, leaving Ruby with the memories and her burning anticipation to keep her company. It was well into the night when she too fell asleep.

She was up at the crack of dawn, cleaning and tidying the house, changing the bed clothes, submerging her real feelings in all the activity. Her mother had baked all day the day before, all the while grumbling, "this should be a wedding cake."

The day seemed to drag on and on never ending, till in her anxiety Ruby started to tidy Larry much too early. By three o'clock both she and Larry were ready and it was only when she thought Fonso was late and checked the clock again, she realised they had at least two hours before the train was due. She realised she was previous indeed. "It must be past May Pen long time and should be at Porus now." She had a cup of tea and waited and waited. It seemed an eternity. "This evening," she prayed, "don't let the train be late."

At about quarter past five the news broke and spread through the district like rainy weather breeze. The train had derailed near Comfort Hall above Balaclava and according to Mr. Young, the village newspaper, "everybody dead – the driver, the conductor, the brakesman and baggage man and all passenger, not a chick nor a chile save."

Ruby received the news as she was on her way to the gate, for Fonso, who was to meet her at the railway station, now came running up the hill. He held her as her body went into spasms with shock – "Oh God, no...oh God, no," Ruby gasped.

Well, they took the decision that they would have to get up to Comfort Hall. He might be dead, again he might not be. He might be injured and need help, and in any case she should be there. Her father agreed and since his car was being fixed, offered to charter a car to take them. He would go too, and Fonso, of course. Her mother, Miss Josie, said she couldn't go – her heart couldn't stand it.

The journey was uneventful. Near the site of the crash the traffic was heavy with trucks, cars, drays, buggies, bicycles and motor bikes with side cars and without, making their way with anxious relatives and friends. The curious, the robbers and pick-pockets moved in also and there was much confusion.

As they made their way across the common to the railway line, the shocked survivors were being assisted by the Salvation Army people from Mandeville. The slightly injured were being given first aid. Those needing further attention were being hustled off to hospital. The dead bodies, such as were recovered, were lying on the raised banking, covered with newspaper and any other material at hand. Some were beyond recognition, some in pieces, all bloody.

They walked among the groaning, moaning mass with Ruby holding on to Fonso for support. It was now daylight. They had been at this since they arrived before midnight. A group of church ladies from a nearby district arrived with two donkeys loaded with tea, coffee and bread for whoever needed it – rescuers and injured survivors alike. Fonso suggested that Ruby take a rest and get some of the coffee but she would not listen. By eight o'clock she had retraced her steps and surveyed the dead and injured several times. Lorenzo was nowhere to be seen. The officer in charge of the operation showed her the list of those taken to hospital – he was not on the list. "Well," he said, "the only thing I can say is that he was not on the train, or," he paused, "he is under that coach we haven't been able to lift yet. The crane will be here shortly though."

Ruby's heart sank. She thought, "if he's under there, he's dead."

Her father and Fonso persuaded her to sit on the stone wall, rest awhile, take it easy and try to be calm. There was nothing else she could do. Fonso got them some coffee and they waited. Nearby, groups of people prayed, sobbed, talked, consoled, eagerly awaiting the arrival of the crane.

Ruby couldn't believe some of the stories she was hearing, of the most ghoulish robberies in the early hours following the crash before the police and military arrived. Scores of men looted the wreckage, stealing anything of value, jewellery, watches, money, luggage, anything. Injured helpless victims were pulled from the wreckage, only to have their valuables taken, sometimes in the most brutal manner. One boy told of a lady who, trapped beneath the wreckage, managed to free her left hand and beckon to a passerby. He immediately tried to pull her rings off, and failing to do so, promptly took out a knife and severed her finger with the rings.

By now the moaning and sobbing had subsided and the crane arrived, and the men hurriedly and methodically proceeded to lift the overturned coach. What was beneath it was as expected. About a dozen people were trapped beneath the coach. It didn't take long to realise they were all dead, some mutilated beyond recognition. As soon as it was safe, people moved nearer under the watchful eyes of the soldiers and police. Ruby, supported by Fonso, surveyed the scene.

In a flash she tore herself from him and darted to the far side with a wail that came from deep down inside her broken heart. Lying on his side was unmistakably her child's father, looking as if he were asleep. "Lorenzo." She spoke his name and bent down to raise his head. He opened his eyes for a second, smiled at her – "Ruby" – and was at peace. Ruby's body shook with sobs. Her father too joined them. A young policeman with a clip board and pen approached.

"You related to him?"

"Yes," Fonso answered.

"What's his name?"

"Lorenzo Davis," Fonso said without looking up.

"You sure?"

"Yes," Fonso said.

The young officer took a piece of cardboard from the clip board, wrote "Lorenzo Davis", attached it to the dead man's feet with a string and beckoned to two men with a stretcher – "Over here."

Ruby, sobbing, looked up as the two men turned him over and attempted to lift him to the stretcher they had placed beside him. In his left hand, still now hidden by his body, he clutched the engine of a red toy train.

Table of Gold

"**G**old – Miss Conse, real gold?"

"Yes, Aunt Clar, solid, solid gold."

"Cho, Miss Conse, you too wonderful, me no believe that."

Miss Conse was positive. She was telling Aunt Clar the story she said her Gang Gang told her many years ago when she was a little girl.

"According to mi Great Granny, it was solid gold, a glisten like the sun so you scarcely could look at it, more shiny than Miss Ada married ring and you know how that shine on a Saturday afternoon." They both laughed heartily.

Miss Ada was the lady who cleaned the brass in the Anglican church and her wedding ring had become a proverb in the district. It is said that when she cleaned the

brass each Saturday she also cleaned her wedding ring, so that, as it was not real gold, it would keep shiny. Matter of fact it was said that that was the reason she offered to clean the brass every week. Every Saturday afternoon she would flash the ring to make sure you saw it, but if you caught her in the middle of the week, she would try to hide the ring so you wouldn't notice it getting dull.

The discussion at hand, however, concerned the story that ever so often surfaced in the village about the gold table that came up out of the water in the big pond on Busha Fenton's property way in the bush. You really couldn't get the truth as the story varied according to the teller, and there were as many versions as there were relatings.

One thing they all agreed on was that at varying intervals a gold table, laden with all manner of golden vessels as if set for a feast, would come up out of the pond, only to disappear again to its bottomless depths. It would remain on the surface for long periods if undisturbed, but would suddenly disappear at the slightest noise or movement, and the legend says that many people spent many nights quietly hiding in the bushes nearby waiting for the table to surface, just to catch a glimpse of this fantastic sight.

The story most heard concerned the man who tried to draw the table out of the pond and lost his life and the animals he used. That is the story Miss Conse was relating to Aunt Clar as they waited on the morning train that would take them to Balaclava.

According to Miss Conse's version, old Busha Fenton owned all the land for miles around. He was a young man when he came to the area after he inherited the land from an old relative, several generations back, who it was said was one of the soldiers that helped Oliver Cromwell capture

Jamaica from the Spaniards, and who, like so many others was given land in Jamaica as payment. As the story goes, one of his workers told him that there was this great big pond on the property far in the bushes, in which they had lost several heads of cattle which usually strayed over to the pond especially in the dry mid-year season when most of the other water holes on the property dried out or were very low. The great pond never went dry, but when the water dried up around the edges, a mud rim was created all around which was dry and hard at the outer edge but the closer you got to the water, the softer and hence the more treacherous it would be. The animals often got into difficulty trying to reach the water. Since the pond was so remote they would sink in the soft mud and die before help could reach them. The stories, however, attributed their drowning to the "well known fact" that whatever controlled the gold table was responsible for luring the thirsty animals to their death.

Now the story was being retold for the umpteenth time by someone who heard it from someone who heard it from someone else.

"A no one or two cow and mule drown there you know Busha D." Busha D was the present owner, being the only surviving male in a long line of Fentons.

"Something een deh," Maas Hezekiah, the Penner, asserted. "You have a time when not even bird fly over deh sah; an you have another time when the pond roll like thunder and the gold table come up with all sorts of newtencils in bright gold set out pon it. So my granny say, but I never really see it."

Busha enquired, "Did your grandmother ever see it herself?"

Maas Hezekiah said no, according to the old lady she heard the story from her grandmother who had heard it from her great-aunt, who had said someone in her family saw it. "Sometime when you seet and talk, bad things happen to you and sometime when it come up and one summady happen to seet, by the time them run go tell other people, and dem reach a di pon' it gone."

"Really?" Busha asked.

Maas Hezekiah continued, "Yes sir, dem say one time them get a obeah woman to come keep a meeting and try to find out who or what was dere, my dear Busha, the woman dance and chant, dance and chant till all of a sudden she stop braps, start tremble and stare into the pond and tear down the narrow pathway deh scream like a wile hog whey got shot. Dem never see her again. She disappear in the pon."

Busha was intrigued. "Well I hope I see your gold table one day and find out where it comes from."

"Some say a old Spaniard leave it deh when the English was coming, and set spirit fi guard it. Some say is the Arawak dem or some people before them, some say is African slave, me don't know, but me hear say one Busha, long long time gone set man fi hide and watch fi di table, and dem watch for months an nottin no gwan, until one night the moon full and the sky cloudy, the two man dem whey a watch hear the pond start roll like thunder and den dem see the table cum up plain as ever."

"One of dem set off fi go call the Busha, and him come wid a heap a man and draft mule and myso cow. One man swim out in a di miggle of the pond and tie on a stout rope round the table - and the driver wid him whip start to lick the animal dem. It look like the table coming out of the water, but all of a sudden a rolling start and the table start sink and di heap a mule and cow whey tie to the table start sink too, till the whole of dem swallow up eena the pon'. Di man dem try to cut the rope but dem wasn't swif' enough – cow and mule and rope drown."

"The Busha claim there was not enough mule and cow. So dem set up again and dis time him put three times di amount of animal and the same thing happen, only dis time it teck four man too, including the white backra overseer that was directing the man dem."

Maas Hezekiah went on to say that, after that, none of the workers would go near the pond, not even to rescue the unfortunate animals who strayed there. The Busha had to put a fence around it, the remnants of which, up to then, could still be seen. Busha D remembered that he had seen a couple of posts and part of the fence and had made a mental note to check on it, but had quite forgotten.

"An Busha, take mi foolish advice and put back the fence sah."

"You know Busha, people say the place deh haunted you know sah, certain time all kind of groaning and antics take place there," Maas Hezekiah related.

Busha was curious, "Have you ever seen any such things there Hezekiah?"

"No, Busha, me no go deh sah."

"Oh Hezekiah, I didn't know you were such a coward."

Maas Hezekiah chuckled and adjusted the cutokoo on his wide shoulder, "Ahi Busha, coward man keep sound bone, dats why mi live so long, no gold table nah get me fi ris' my life."

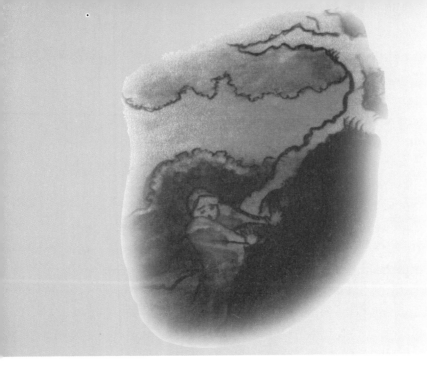

To Rahtid

You know there are some people who just must show off no matter where they are and who they are among. Show off born in them like toenail, hair or fingernail. And they find every opportunity to display themselves to gain what I don't know, for they only succeed in showing up their ignorance and stupidity to the annoyance and disgust of everybody else.

Like cross roads and cotton tree, post office and school, Chiney shop, church and rum bar – there is always one such crosses in each district. You take that big mouth boy working with Busha Farquharson as farrier or groom, or horseboy as some people style him, for very few persons called him by his right name Alphonso or Phonso for short.

This young man, quite personable, strong and well built, was a perfect show off and, on top of that, a bully, provoking and downright obnoxious.

He took great delight interfering with everybody, always finding something to laugh at in other people and to ridicule them. He laughed at everything and anything: Miss Iris' lisp, Mother P's bandy legs, at Jessie Morgan because she stuttered and little Beryl because she was at that stage when she lost her front teeth. He even made sport of Baada Ellis because of his deep bass singing voice, though everybody else loved to hear Baada sing. Nobody escaped his ridiculing and nobody would do anything about him, maybe because he was so big and strong, and strong man can't wrong.

He took particular pleasure in taunting and poking fun at Chin the Chinese shopkeeper, at the way he walked, the way he talked, and he always announced his arrival in the shop with "Serve, Chiney Chin Pong Yaah", followed by more mock Chinese speech, pretending to converse in Chinese and to sing in Chinese. He knew a lot about Chiney people, he frequently told his hearers, including Chin and his family. They were weak because he said they ate too much rice, nasty for they ate dog meat. He also knew about the intimate parts of their body and their sexual behaviour and he often called out in Chin's hearing – "Chiney nyam dog." He told everyone not to call the shopkeeper no Mister Chin, "Just call him plain Chin, for when dem come yah dem count two fi one."

His behaviour annoyed and angered Chin to no end, but he met all the insults and jeers with stony silence, serving him his few purchases, ignoring the tormenting until...

111

Phonso also behaved quite abominably to the young women and young girls of the district. It was as if they all belonged to him, his property. He loudly called out their names from across the road especially if there were other people around to hear him address them in the most suggestive ways, and if they ignored him as they most often than not did, he would tell his hearers what he had done with them on some previous occasion, including the night before, or what he was going to do to them tonight. Surprisingly no one took him to court though many of his utterances warranted it.

"Duppy know who to frighten", so the saying goes, so he was sensible enough to leave certain young ladies alone, like the head teacher's two daughters, Custos's niece and Busha's young sister, and Chin's two daughters born to his half-black, half-Indian wife. That must have been difficult for him for they were blessed with the best features of both father and mother and as Corporal was heard to often remark, "prettier than any money", and indeed their father guarded them as he did his money. The story went around the district that they, according to Chinese custom, were promised to two brothers, the sons of a rich merchant in Kingston.

Alphonso continued to heckle Chin, and Chin continued to ignore him. This went on for such a long time that Phonso was convinced that Chin was afraid of him... until one day he came into the shop to find Jasmine, the younger and prettier of the two, alone at the counter. He had been waiting for just this kind of chance. Making sure there was no one else in the shop, he began to make subtle and lewd passes at the shy girl, as the saying goes, putting argument to the girl. She of course paid no attention to his advances, silently going about getting the items that he asked for, and he in his conceit took her silence to mean that she didn't mind, or perhaps even liked it, for according to his warped mind "ah so woman stay". So the devil kicked him, and he was so taken up with the girl, he did not see her father sitting on a chair hidden by the half open door leading to their living quarters at the back of the shop. All this time the girl was serving the items he requested without saying a word.

As he handed her the money and she reached out to take it, he grabbed her arm, pulling her towards him, and with his other hand took hold of her right breast, and resting his elbow on the counter pushed himself up on to the counter and was about to plant a kiss on the frightened girl, who made not a sound.

In one motion, and with lightning speed unseen by Phonso, Chin was over the counter on the customer side and, taking hold of Phonso's two legs, hauled him to the ground shouting, "Sol a bitch."

Completely taken by surprise, Phonso struggled to his feet as Chin landed two kicks in rapid succession to his abdomen, doubling Phonso at his middle, knocking the breath out of him and before he could catch back his breath, Chin quickly caught his left arm and in one deft move hurled the breathless Phonso from the shop to the piazza.

Now on his feet and in a rage, Phonso advanced to Chin, "Yu Chiney rass, ah gwine kill yu tiday."

By this time people on their way to work at the sugar factory stopped to see what was happening. Some of the women shouted, "No Phonso, no, yu gwine get yuself in trouble." They were sure this big bull would make a hash of the small-bodied middle-aged shop keeper, as he had done with all who challenged him in a fight. No one was prepared for what happened next, and they watched in horror as

Phonso advanced on Chin. Miss Conse, who was one of the first on the scene shouted, "Lawd God im dead now, run Chin run."

He ran, only as far as the "salt-ting" counter where a small pudding pan held pickle-salt for customers. With customary lightning speed, Chin emptied the contents of the pan in the face of the advancing Phonso, blinding him with the salt water.

Now Phonso was really mad and described how he was going to make "joncrow meat" out of Chin. By the time he could open his eyes, Chin was on the flat ground waiting, feet apart, his hands in a peculiar formation looking rather like a monkey. Phonso lunged at him with all his weight. Chin nimbly stepped aside and planted a well timed kick in Phonso's groin, forcing him to the ground. Yelling in pain and uttering a string of forty shilling words, he was on his feet again moving towards Chin, his fists at the ready. But Chin stood his ground, evading the blows with practised skill, and with equal skill, planted damaging blows to choice parts of Phonso's body and soon had him in trouble once more.

Phonso managed, in the sparring that followed, to get a hold of his right arm, and was in the act of pulling Chin to him, his head ready to deliver the deathly butt for which he had become famous. With his other hand, Chin held on to him, and in one movement pulled him off his feet, throwing him over, and sent him sprawling on his back. The growing crowd was in shock. "Is Chiney science man dis to rahtid," one man remarked. They couldn't believe that the village bully, the district strong man was getting the beating of his life from, of all persons, the weak little Chin.

Once more Phonso was on his feet, shame, rage and embarrassment killing him. From a nearby dray he pulled a

piece of stick about six feet long and as he advanced on Chin the crowd shouted, "No Phonso no." Mother P bawled out, "Lawd mi God, im dead now, call Corporal." With all the strength he could summon, he made a swipe at Chin's head with the stick and missed as Chin ducked. Once more Phonso aimed and swiped. He missed again as Chin caught the end of the stick, speedily disarming him.

He moved towards Chin bellowing like a bull, head down, arms out-stretched, ready it seemed to devour Chin who, with the stick, gave him a solid blow across his belly, knocking the breath out of him, and as he stumbled Chin placed the stick between his moving legs, sending him clean across the road where his head collided with the culvert, and he was out like a light.

By this, the astonished crowd was shouting and cheering. Miss Conse with some delight, remarked, "Yes Phonso meet im match tiday...An look who disapline im... Missa Chin, yu do well...Ah bet im don't fast wid no baddy again."

Amid the congratulations and applause and commendations, Chin exclaimed, "Sol a bitch," calmly walked back to his shop, picked up his feather duster and began dusting his shelves, not uttering another word.

Phonso moved away from the district and from that day the Chiney man, Chin, was known as Mister Chin to all.

By Duty Bound

"**M**adam, sell mi two poun a brown rice, and quarter poun a salt fish. Mi de pon hase".

With the back of her hand she hurriedly wiped the tears that were rolling down her cheeks and answered, "Comin."

She had been, for the last few minutes, crying quietly behind the bread case where she could not be seen, as she had been doing for some time now, since she heard the news.

She picked up the end of her large apron and wiped her face as she moved to the counter to tend the waiting customer. Things had been a little slow in the village shop that day as it always was on a Tuesday. The children were

at school and her husband had gone since last night, ostensibly "to buy goods" in the parish capital about thirty miles away.

This was so for a few years now. At first he would leave very early on the morning diesel train and return late evening with the truck that brought the goods. Nowadays he left from the night before, returning next evening. She thought nothing of it until she discovered, not by chance, that her husband had a brown skinned lover with whom he had a four year old son. He had rented a place for her to live in her cousin's house in the town where he could go and come as he pleased. By all accounts, whenever he left to buy goods for their prosperous shop, he would spend the night with his young lover.

She didn't question him, even after she received a letter setting out the story of the relationship. She couldn't read the letter herself. She was later to learn that it was written by the girl in question. Her good friend, the village midwife who had delivered her five children, read the letter and explained the position to her. She said nothing, and her friend was surprised to see that she displayed no emotion whatever at the news. But whenever she was alone, like today, she secretly cried. No one ever saw her tears, not her husband nor any of the children.

She couldn't understand why her husband needed to take another woman. In the old country when the wife bore no male child the husband was free to find a woman to give him the precious male offspring which would ensure that the family name would live on and which the wife would rear as her own child or children. Matter of fact, wives often encouraged this and on some occasions would themselves pick the woman. But she had borne three boys and two girls and in her reckoning all should have been well in that regard.

What is more, since her arrival from China fifteen years ago, she had worked extremely hard to build up the business. Sun up to sundown she was in the shop attending to customers, making sure the shop was neat and tidy and, in between, cooking all the meals for the family. Each night after the shop was closed, she spent hours wrapping, chopping, cleaning, packing, weighing, preparing for the next day. At the crack of dawn she was up frying codfish fritters, with batter set up from the night before. They were a favourite of the villagers and they sometimes lined up to purchase these delicious fritters. From an open window each day she served their morning supplies of tea and bread and cocoa and sugar to those on their way to the fields and the sugar factory nearby. Her husband would be up a couple hours later, and soon after lunch, would take a nap for at least an hour.

This did not go unnoticed by the villagers, as Miss Conse was heard to comment, "Madam no easy yu know, she can work just like any Jamaican woman." Everyone knew how hard she worked and that she did not complain about the hard work. The villagers knew too that her husband was not the hardest working person they knew.

All day long Madam served in the shop, on her feet serving, working, pausing only long enough to prepare family meals and to hurriedly eat her share. She made and mended clothes for her children, seeing to their comfort and well being in every need. She never complained. She was always at her husband's beck and call, ready to supply his every wish, ready to provide for his every whim. When she had her babies she spent no more than a few days in bed. She worked every waking hour to the neglect of her own deteriorating health. She did all this work without a word, without a murmur. Blue varicose veins now appeared on both legs.

Madam even blamed herself for her husband's unfaithful action, wondering what she had neglected to do, where she had failed. In her maturity she was still a handsome, strong woman, a little plump, but by no means unattractive. Quietly and alone she bore the pain of the discovery of her husband's infidelity.

Today he came home, bringing her a jade ring which made her heart leap with joy and love. Then after he had eaten his favourite meal she had diligently prepared in anticipation of his return, he told her about his affair, his lover and his young son. She quietly wept and for the first time he saw her tears. She was sure he was about to leave her for his lover, as his cousin had done, and she braced herself for that bitter news. But that was not the purpose of the telling. He announced that he was bringing home the child who was just two months older than her last child, also a boy.

That, to her, was better. He was not leaving and she was stunned but relieved. She would have him to help her raise all the children. The jade ring, she smiled, was a peace offering. Having another to take care of was not really a problem and she knew she could manage. She knew she was bound by tradition and conditioned by her own feelings. Accordingly, her husband's child was her own, no question about that, she would raise the child according to custom and tradition, and she vowed that she would, as best she could, regard him as such.

She sat in stony, tearful silence as he told her the whole story, assuring her that she and all the children were his responsibility and that he would do all in his power to care for them. When he had finished speaking she looked at him, and speaking quietly and firmly, gave him the promise that she would take care of all the children, making no distinction between them. But there were two conditions, first he must break totally with his lover. That was easy for she was about to join her parents in America to continue her studies, so she would be out of the way. The second condition was even easier. He must not let the children know who the mother was, they would be told that he had adopted the child who was really a cousin, but who, by the custom of adoption in China, was their brother and must be treated as such.

With that agreement, they resumed their life as if it were the most natural thing in the world, and she carried on as before without protest, without complaining. As it turned out, the boy was the image of his little brother and as a matter of fact, they looked very much like twins. When she told the details to her friend, the midwife, and of her decision based on her culture and heritage, her friend could only remark, "You Chinese women are something else. Is a good thing is you and not me."

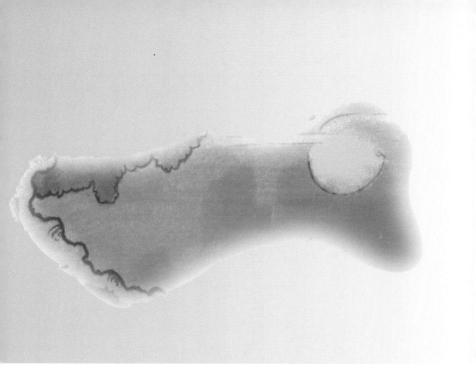

Gilnock Race Horse

Old Lennon took his place
on the long bench
in Mister Chin's private bar
across from Maas Luther and Brother Jack
Uncle Sam and Mister Roden
beside him was Baba C
Maas Bulla and Mister Ankle
it was their regular Friday-evening spree
when they exchanged all manner of stories
while they consumed round after round
of their favourite white proof rum.
For the past hour they were at it
until the talk got around to race horses.

After downing his second Q of whites
he took the floor.

"You think now-a-days horse can run?
Dem yah horse a donkey cubby
when yu put dem side by side wid ole time horse.
When me was a likkle bwoy inna short trousis
my father used to carry mi go a Gilnock
fi watch horse race pon a holiday.
From day jus a light we leave home
when we reach near Santa
the road busy with horse and buggy
few moto car an truck
nuff walk foot man
everybody heading for Gilnock race course.
Some have tings fi sell by di gate
Yu si horse of all description an class an condition
under shady-tree, under bood under shed
still more horse a come een.
By the time race fi start
mus be bout a tousen a dem ready fi run.
ah so di horse dem
ah so di people
di big shot dem dress up
inna coatie tail and top hat
an di few lady dem inna bustle
shif tilta petticoat shawl
an tight button up shoes
wid broad hat an parasol.
Den di bettin start
man a bet shillin, two-an-six
five shillin, ten shillin
Busha an di odder rich man dem a bet guinea
big bet, likkle bet

two to one, five to one
ten to one and twenty to one
di place busy an noisy caan done.

As soon as the bettin set fi every race
di jockey dem mount up
bugle blow an di horse dem gone
roun an roun an roun.
Plenty man gald, nuff man sad
for dem bet dung to dem wife house money
bet what dem can't afford
a poor-show-great.

Well dis race day
I remember it was a Easter Monday
we lef yard before daylight
"Before cock put awn im drawers", as mi Granny sey
an we reach Gilnock when sun hot.
Since mi father nuh have nuff money fi bet
we go roun where di horse dem keep
an listen to what di groom an jockey dem sayin
for if you want to know how to bet a race course
   listen to dem
dem know more dan di owner or anybody.

Well there was a pretty gray mare from Wesmalan
   name Cusho Puss.
Dem match her wid another mare
dat did belong to the owner of the race course
a man name Missa Densha
dem call dat mare Red Gal.
Di bettin was strong on di side a Red Gal
she was definitely di favourite.

Jus as mi father decide to bet on Red Gal
a young man come up an whisper to him,
"Bet on the gray, the gray, bet on the gray."
But mi father no pay him no mine
im say di gray look bruck dung arredy.
Mi was a mischevious likkle bwoy
an as mi father turn im back
mi follow the young man
go roun where dem have di horse dem
mi hear di groom an di jockey dem
talking bout di race
dem say dat Cusho Puss boun fi win
for dem pepper im,
and di supple Jack dat the jockey going to ride
  wid soak inna pepper fi nine days
and when im lick wid dat she gwine fly
like lightning.

Well sir me had ten shilling
mi modder give mi fi buy a Leghorn cock
an is like di devil kick mi
unbeknownst to mi father
mi teck mi modder cock money
an buy not one but two ticket five shillin a piece
fi win offa Cusho Puss.
You can jus imagine
how a nervous when the bugle blow
an di race start and Red Gal
jump into the lead one time.

Before yu know it
dem was comin round di firs turn
an when a look a nearly mess up mi self
Cusho Puss a come dead lass.

Mi say Lord mi modder Leghorn rooster fly gone
she gwine sure to murder mi.
A fret a fret, a fret...so mi a fret
so mi father a call out pon di top a im voice
Red Gall, Red Gal, run Red Gal
Mi can barely call out Cusho Puss Cusho Puss.

All of a sudden as dem come roun fi start di lass lap
the jockey start drop lick wid di pepper switch
an si yah sah
Cusho Puss shoot off dung the track like any bullet.
Shi gallop pass all di odder horse dem
An now she an Red Gal neck an neck
headin toward di winnin post.
Now mi fine mi voise and a shout
Cusho Puss, Cusho Puss, Cusho Puss
Ah bawl till a hoarse...Cusho Puss, Cusho Puss
in di excitement ah think a even cuss a bad word.
Good ting mi father nuh hear.

By dis time di Jockey git up eena di saddle
and drop two bitch lick wid di pepper switch
Cusho Puss shot pass Red Gal
Shot pass di winnin post
An win di race by about six length.
Me glad so tell.
Busha nearly faint way for im bet heavy.
But a yah so di prekke begin
For when di jockey try fi pull up
Cusho Puss wouldn' stop
so di pepper a bun, so di mare a run
di poor jockey couldn stop her.
Di owner nearly mad
a man jump pon a horse

125

an try fi catch dem
but haffi give up an turn back
Im couldn catch dem
di mare a gallop same way.
Some likkle bwoy in a mango tree
start chant out
"Horse a gallop an di man caan pull im back
ride im jockey ride im bwoy."

Yu never si so much excitement from yu born
some time after dat
wi hear say dat di jockey manage fi slip off a im
somewhere dung a Santa Battam
widout any serious injury
and Cusho Puss never stop gallop
till im reach im owna yard way dung a Wesmalan
dem fine im din nex day still saddle up
under the guango tree whey dem usually tie im.
Ahi; Ah say dat was a day.

Say you want to know what happen to di ticket dem me buy?
Mi tell mi father bout di ticket dem
An is di first time mi father ever hug mi up.
Wi collect the winnings
Seven poun ten shillings.
Im give mi five shilling fi myself,
an a reach heaven same time
Im teck one poun fi himself
an him an im fren dem drink up
wi buy di rooster fi mi modder
an a hen to match for brawta
and nuff tings fi mi likkle sista.

We reach home dat night full a food an liquor
an my father meck mi promise
not to do anything like dat again
an im promise not to tell mi modder.
Dat was di secret between di two a wi fi life.
From dat day mi an him was best a fren
specially when im teck some a di money
an buy a pretty likkle heffer calf fi mi
ascorden to him to meck mi into a man.

But if a live till a dead
I will never forget dat day
mi father a call out fi Red Gal
Red Gal...run Red Gal
an me a bawl out Cusho Puss
Cusho Puss run Cusho Puss
an di likkle bwoy dem in di mango tree
"Horse a gallop and di man caan pull im back
ride im jockey ride im bwoy."

Childhood Smells

I recall oh so well
The pleasant smell of mangoes
Sweet limes and orange rind
Sweet pineapples
And sugar cane fresh reaped
Lying heaped up in the days hot sun
Rose apples we searched to find
By the fun pond and the bees
We had to fight off from
The naseberries granddad hid
in the tall guinea grass
knowing we were specially fond of these
Then there were the kitchen smells
Our aunt holiday cooking fried fish
To be eaten with fresh cassava bammie
The enticing Saturday gungo peas soup
The lure the tempting odour
of pot roast beef on Sunday
And back home
There was Father in his hakka kitchen
And the smells oh so different
But no less enticing and delicious
Roast chicken with five spice
Pork roasted or stewed with pickled mustard
And corned fish fragrant tasty pungent nice
Heung as he termed it
Not for the timid and snooty
But great with fresh cooked rice ...
Oh those smells of childhood
Lifetime memories.

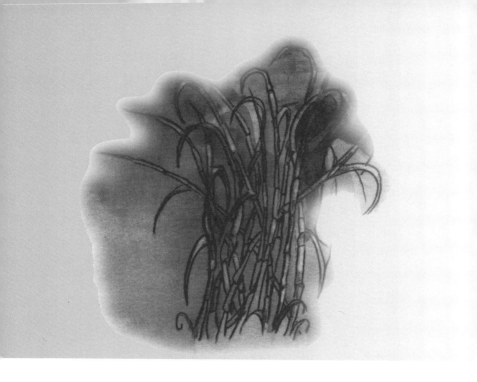

Golden Shower

"**M**eck a tell you somthing, if Hyacinth did know that Maas Ferdie would come back so quick then she woulda never allow Gladstone to follow her home from the function that night, and if Maas Charley didn't get vex with Maas Josh and quarrel with him, and if Aunt Floss didn't interfere, and if Maas Claude didn't intervene, and if mi mother didn't send mi to take a message to Maas Ferdie…if, if…and if Mr. Beal did…if, if, if and more if…if Miss Bell never mad she would turn teacher, this if…if…if.

But the whole afternoon at the ball groung well into the evening into night when the dancing start, Gladstone eyeing Hyacinth and vice versa – and by the time it reach nine o'clock, the two of them was at fever pitch – and it was as if by arrangement Hyacinth decide to leave; she just knew Gladstone would follow her. In the height of the excitement she slipped Aunty and hurried home to the house where she lived alone with her grandfather, Maas Ferdie, right next door to we. She just knew Gladstone was not far behind; she could feel him.

Gladstone on the other hand just feel the magnet. As Hyacinth turn through the school gate he was behind her at a safe enough distance so nobody would suspect, because if anybody suspect, the story would come out and there would be hell to pay.

So all along the quarter mile of roadway down to the house he kept well to the bankside and in the dark. At one point he thought somebody was following him. He stopped, waited a few seconds peering into the dark. There was no one. So he ventured on. Little further when he heard Peter and Ernest coming in the opposite direction, plucking out a tune on the banjo, he slid into the culvert and waited till when they were at a safe distance up the road. He hurried on and arrived at Hyacinth's gate just in time to see her go through the front door from the little varandah, and he hid behind the guango tree and waited. She lit the lamp and came back into the varandah and covered up the parrot cage.

He was certain she was looking towards the tree. Expectant like, she hesitated a purposely long moment and moved inside. Gladstone's heart sank as he saw her close the door. Once more, she paused to look through the glass in the door towards the tree – and then she moved deliberately and with purpose to the other side of the varandah, pulled the latch and pushed up the sash window, and disappeared.

Gladstone reckoned that she went into the room from which her room was supposed to open, and he waited until the lamp was lit in her room, then he made his move. In an instant he was under the window, making sure that no one was watching him. He reached up and gripped the window sill with both hands, pulled himself up, bracing his right foot on the wall, and before you could quint he was inside the dining room.

Hyacinth's room adjoined this to the back and the connecting door was open. Gladstone waited, not sure what to do next, and then he heard, 'In here.' Quickly and quietly he crossed the room and was standing beside Hyacinth's bed foot. She was reclining on the pillows just looking. He stretched out his arms and Hyacinth took hold and pulled herself up to him. It seemed as if all her twenty-three years and his twenty were waiting for this moment. There was nothing to be said, for both had gone over this in their minds several times in the previous months, in the previous days, in the previous hours, and so there was no need to say anything. Matter of fact, neither of them could talk, neither had done anything like this before, man and woman business was new to them. But the instinct, the knowing of life and the same man and woman business was the force.

In the heat of the loving they forgot all about Maas Ferdie, and because he had got fed up with the foolish row he was having with his long time friend (because of liquor – beers to be exact. An unusual character in the white rum district, Maas Ferdie could down two dozen beers at a session. His record to date was twenty-eight). Maas Ferdie was home, going up the four cut-stone steps to the varandah – cussing and swearing and generally taking it out on whoever had the misfortune to be in his bad-word range.

He pushed open the front door and called out, "Hya, Hya, light the etna and hot up a cup of coffee fi mi." He was on his way to his room and Hyacinth jumped up, pulled back down her nightie, and answered, 'A comin grandpa,' as she put her hand in the sleeve of the house coat.

"Well stop you coming and come. God damn – stupidness. Sometimes a can't stand Josh, Beal and the whole damn lot a dem..."

Hyacinth wasn't listening. She was busy tying the house coat band as she whispered to Gladstone (who was sitting up in the bed, the sheet pulled over his naked diminishing stiffness, scared out of his wits, because Maas Ferdie would castrate him if he were caught), motioning with her hand, 'put on you clothes and wait. I will tell you when.... Im soon fall asleep and then you can come back een.' She crossed the sitting hall, lit the etna on the little table in the corner of the dining room, put on the coffee pot and moved to the doorway to her grandfather's room.

He was sitting on the bed, taking off his trousers – he had already taken off the boots. He stood up with his long dress shirt covering his big foot calico drawers almost down past his knees trying to get out the cuff links.

'Oh botheration.'

By this, Gladstone was half dressed, peeping through the crack of the door and Hyacinth seized the opportunity, signalled to him to go outside, same time saying to her grandfather, 'meck me help you Gramps.' She blocked his view with her body as she slowly took out the two links, while Gladstone, shirt and shoes in hand (he had managed to get on the pants), crossed the sitting hall and went quietly like a ram puss through the front door to the little garden by the four cut-stone steps and stooped down in the fern bed behind the bell flowers tree, waiting till the old man went to sleep and for another signal from Hyacinth.

Hyacinth went to mix the coffee while Gramps, still grumbling, moved to the varandah, and watching out of the corner of her eye, Hyacinth's heart nearly stop beating. She thought – 'Lord have mercy, 'im goin' see Gladstone.' But those fears proved groundless. He was too drunk.

Well, for months the whole village was talking about the warm bath that Gladstone got that night, crouched down in the garden. For Gramps had had a few beers well, and he had a bad habit of standing on the step and making water on the fern garden when he was under waters. He reached the hedge between the house and the fence as he managed to open his pants front and started to pee pee. Being the age that he was, that stream took longer than normal. Poor Gladstone couldn't move. He had to choose between that and being discovered. He was just able to shift his head so that the golden shower missed his face, but the rest of him – wet from head to foot. Luckily he didn't get on the shirt and shoes, so he was able to keep those dry. But everything else – wet up with recycled Red Stripe Pilsener, delivered to the tune of "When the roll is called up yonder", Maas Ferdie's favourite hymn sung on all occasions, especially at such times.

The ordeal finally ended. But when his friends and foes alike laughed after him as the story circulated for the next few months, they couldn't understand the funny smile on his face, like please puss, for their story ended with the end of the golden shower. They didn't see what took place after the old man fell into the coma of an alcoholic sleep, snoring, sawing board enough to build a church.

In the little back room where she had the big bath pan, Hyacinth took Gladstone and bathed, shampooed and powdered him like a baby, and after the merriment, cuddled him in her arms like a baby, and pomaded and brushed his hair like a baby, and cradled his face between her full breasts like a baby. Well, suffice it to say it was only the crowing of the second, or could be third or fourth cock, if you understand, that sent him off with that smile on his face for which only Hyacinth and he know the reason, and me of course."

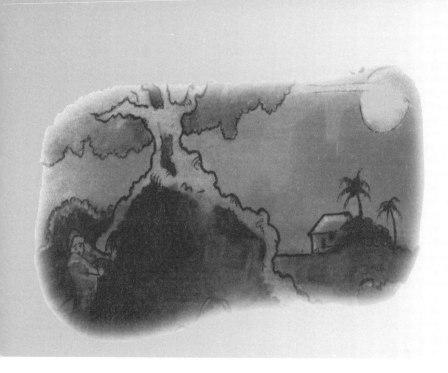

Myal

That Saturday evening in December, market lasted longer than usual. The evening was cool and there was still some food and things to sell and people lingered a little longer than usual. There was a sort of a mood of expectancy as if somewhere in the back of everybody's mind they knew something was up. Something.

Nobody could tell what, but it was there hanging in the air and as if by strange gut feeling, some unexplained reasoning, some instinct, some knowing that no one really could define, people were waiting. Some talking, some looking, some not really doing anything special, almost in slow motion, moving without purpose in a strange eerie suspense, seeing but not seeing, hearing but not really hearing.

So intense was this feeling that no one noticed the four people who had entered the market as brown dusk was creeping over the place. The four ordinary looking men, one much older than the rest, two about middle aged, and the fourth, a young boy about twelve in the peak of puberty, moved to a corner of the market under the eaves of the little wooden building that housed the meat stall, and quietly and slowly uncovered the bundles they carried. That is, the two middle aged men and the young boy. The old man carried no bundle. Over his left shoulder hung a cutakoo, the kind which is often seen on the shoulders of men and women alike, a flat thatch pouch over a foot deep and about ten inches wide with one side forming a lid. A string of plaited thatch held it on the shoulder. From this, the old man took out a pair of sticks about the size of his thumb and a little over a foot long.

The two men each uncovered their bundles to reveal a pair of drums, the type that was rarely seen. From his bundle, the young boy took a small square drum and began to tighten the skin using the pegs at each side. He put the drum down as soon as he was satisfied with the tuning, long enough to take off the pair of rough shoemaker-made shoes he wore, and slapped his naked feet on the bare hard earth.

Miss Constance was the first to notice them. Miss Constance was always the first to notice things. As she opened her mouth to tell Miss Vie, her friend who was standing nearby, it began. There was no need for her to say anything, the old man's voice in a strange pitch started a melody they had not all heard before and the other two men simultaneously started a rhythm on their drums, held it for a while and then the boy joined in. The music was slow and deliberate and seemed to be some kind of chant. Not surprising, as they were said to come from a district not too far down the road on the way to Maggotty, just below Appleton after the deep bend and where the road straightened past the fourth mile post. They were myal people who were said to be associated with the spirit world.

"Me don't business wid dat you know Miss Vie, me is a godfearing woman and me and all dem obeah and duppy business don't tek tea." It was Miss Constance as usual who had the first say.

Miss Vie was a little less harsh. "Well mam, every man to him own order according to St. Paul."

But Miss Constance was not about to be so tolerant. "You see me now mam, if me had the power dem don't come out into the public wid dem tings you know, dem should be banned for it is evil, a stop should be put to dem."

As if the men were hearing, the tune had come to an end and the singing and the drumming stopped. For a moment, Miss Constance couldn't make up her mind whether it was what she said that had caused the stoppage, and just as she was about to continue, the singing and the drumming resumed. This time, the old man was using the pair of sticks to assist the rhythm on the edge of one of the drums and the young boy had put down his drum and was standing beside him.

Miss Constance observed, "Is dance him gwine to dance Miss Vie." By this, all the people in the market were gathered around the group. The boy slapped his bare feet against the ground three times, knelt and kissed the ground, slapped the ground with his bare palms and the dance started. Slow at first, then gradually intensifying, now with the drums leading him on. Now he leads the drummers, weaving patterns of movement with his feet, his arms, his head, his whole body, pelvis, shoulders. The rhythm possessed his body and he moved now like a bull, now like a snake, a bird, a mongoose, a horse. It seemed that he took the shapes and movements of all the animals. It was so strangely beautiful.

Those watching stood riveted to the spot as the young dancer carved these images in the space around him. He seemed unconscious now and seemed too to soar above the heads of all who watched. But his feet never left the ground and now he began a whirl that continued for minutes, it appeared, until he fell to the ground, his hands slapping the skins of the two drums in a final beat.

Immediately, the old man threw down the sticks and held the boy's head between his knees as he stood astride the now limp body. The boy looked at the old man and said in a clear precise voice, "dog a nyam dog."

The old man shook the boy. "Wha kine a dog?"

The boy's voice was softer now, "Woman dawg, brown woman dawg."

With that, his head slipped from between the old man's knees and he appeared lifeless as the old man laid him on the ground. From his pocket, the old man took a flask of white rum and rubbed first his own face and then the boy's. From his cutakoo he took a shack-shack made from a ground gourd and began a new rhythm – slow, haunting. After a few moments, the boy opened his eyes, sat up and looked as he did when he first entered the market that evening.

Everyone's eyes were on the boy as he moved now to where a group of men were watching, among them the Custos whose wife was lying desperately ill. She had seen all the doctors that it was possible to see and just that evening the specialist from Kingston had informed Custos that there was nothing they could do for his wife, it would be only a few days, weeks at most, and she would die. No one knew this except the Custos who had read the letter that his bearer had brought only an hour or so ago on the evening train. He was visibly moved when the young dancer said to him for all to hear, "Custos, your wife is very ill. The doctors give her over. They don't know what is wrong, and is just as well, they can't help her."

Custos was stunned. The voice sounded like the specialist from Kingston.

"But this can't be, this is the boy from the district down the road."

"Yes Custos, and she will die in a few days, weeks at most."

This is incredible, thought the Custos, he is almost quoting the letter word for word and in the doctor's voice.

"How do you know this boy? How?"

The boy smiled. "I can see Custos, I can see the letter you just get."

"What else did the letter say?"

"It also say that since there is no chance, he would recommend that you take her home so she can die in peace among the people she loves and who love her."

Custos couldn't believe his ears.

"And there's another thing sir, he says that your friend Mr. Phillips has paid the bill at the laboratory so you don't owe anything there."

This boy has extraordinary powers, I wonder if he can help her, Custos thought. People like him were not supposed to believe in all that kind of thing, it's not for him at all, but he was desperate. He had done everything he could and all that was in vain. The most precious person in the world to him was about to die and he could do nothing to help. In his desperation he said to the boy, "Since you know so much, do you know what is the matter with her?"

"No sir, but I can find out."

"How, boy, how?"

"We have to talk in private sir."

The old man who was listening to all this explained to Custos that this boy had special gifts. He communicates with the spirits through his dance and the spirits tell him the messages. That is why they were in the market today. The spirits had directed them to come to the market as that was the place where they would learn the truth they were seeking about a man that was also mysteriously ill. The fact that his wife lived nearby was the reason why he had got a message for her also.

"Can you help my wife, son?"

"We have to talk in private Custos," the old man said solemnly.

He knew that it was not the right thing by his standards, people in his society did not believe in that sort of thing, but he really couldn't think of that now, he just had to try one last thing. He beckoned to the old man, "Come this way," and led him along with the boy over the paved steps of the shop piazza across the driveway of his house and offered them a seat on the verandah.

"Well, is like this Custos, the spirits help us when we ask them. They are the spirits of we old relatives that gone before. Through the dance we contact them and they tell us what to do. If they can help they tell we, if they can't they let us know too. Whichever way, we know and we know what to do."

"How did this young man get the power?" Custos asked, still a little doubtful.

"Well sir," the old man continued, "the spirits choose you if they think you are worthy. In every generation they find one. My grandson here is really the chosen one but we support him with the music and the other things."

"But that makes him very powerful, he could be wealthy."

The old man shook his head. "No my dear Custos, the powers are only to be used for good, never evil. If anyone try to use them for wrong doings and for selfish purpose the power will just go. As it come, so it go. You see Custos, those that don't understand think we are obeah workers. That is far from the truth as east is from west, we can help to put things right, we can't use these powers for anything that is evil or bad."

"Can you help my wife? I will pay you anything you ask."

Again the old man smiled. "Thank you kindly Custos but that also is forbidden, we can't take money. The spirits would be displeased and would do serious things to us. We can only ask for what is necessary for the duty at hand, nothing more. If after the job is done you want to give the boy a present, then he will have to go back to the spirits and get permission to accep' it."

Custos couldn't believe all this, but he was so desperate. "All right then, what should I do?"

The old man conferred with the boy whose only response was to nod his head. To each suggestion he nodded in assent. The old man turned back to Custos.

"Well sir, if you wish he will dance for your wife. He will need a nightgown wear by your wife that is not wash. In other words, same as she take it off he has to get it before it is washed, and something in the house, a little thing like a trinket that she love, something that belong to her."

Custos said, "That is easy, she has a little toy cat that she loves and used to keep by her bedside on the table, and I will get the nightgown."

The boy who, up to now, remained silent said, "Please Custos, we don't have much time".

"I know son, we will work as fast as we can."

After another short conference with the boy, the old man said, "We will have to do the duty by Monday evening latest, before midnight."

The old man and boy returned to their companions who had been waiting and said, "Come, we have plenty work to do, we have to pray soul Monday evening, same place yah so."

They were off to their home and Custos moved with the speed of a man possessed and before half an hour had passed he was on his way to Kingston. He had made his mind up, people could say what they wanted. The woman who was his life, who had been his one and only love since they were teen children, was dying and anything he could do would be done. He would bring her home. After all, what did he have to lose. And people did talk. Many were sympathetic, many totally surprised that a man like Custos should fall prey to what they called "workers of iniquity". Preachers on Sunday spoke out against the decision to have the myal people search for healing for his wife. Parson was very upset but since Custos did not really belong to his church he didn't have much to say.

Miss Constance was perhaps the most vocal. "I am surprised at Custos. He should never do a thing like that."

Miss Vie her friend reasoned, "But Miss Conse, suppose it was you."

"Matters not," said Miss Conse, but Miss Vie was a practical lady. "Well I guess you can talk now, you don't have a loved one on dying. Who have dry peas look fi fire you hear Miss Conse."

While the debate continued, some for and some against, all day Sunday and all day Monday the old man and his friends worked to get things ready for Monday night. They had requested and obtained the material they required from Custos. By Sunday night Custos arrived back home with his wife who had to be lifted by four men to her bed from the car. She was a large lady and the men had a tough time but they managed. All her friends came to see her for what they were convinced was the last time. She recognised no one, not even her own sons and little grand-daughter whom everyone knew was the apple of her eye. The fact that she was dying made the whole district sad. She was a good woman, well loved for her charity and caring for the poor and needy.

By twilight the crowd began to gather in the market. The news had gone the rounds that there was going to be some excitement in the market that night and people were not about to miss the happening. So by the time it was dark, the little market was already crowded. Even those who were against the ceremony rubbed shoulders with those who were for it. Others just came for the entertainment with no particular feeling one way or the other. The truck that Custos had sent for them arrived carrying the men and others of their group, in all about fifteen persons, and they alighted from the truck and waited for the old man, their leader, to be lifted down by one of the young men. Then the boy dancer moved from the end nearest to the front of the truck carrying a large object concealed under a floral cloth. He was helped down from the truck and he and the group moved to the centre of the market. The covered object was placed on the ground. The drummers were ready. The two items requested, the nightgown and the toy cat, were brought to the old man. Shortly after, when all was in readiness, the singing and the drumming started, and soon the dance.

Once more the boy moved over the hard earth like water, effortlessly, dancing to the drums and the singing for hours it seemed with nothing really happening. The crowd was just beginning to get anxious when the boy moved to the old man who was standing beside the drummers, beckoned to him and took the two items the old man knowingly offered. The drummers now following the lead of the dancer increased the pace and dancer and drummers began what seemed to be a competition of speed, yet in perfect coordination. The dancer now leaped several times back and forth over the covered object he had placed in the centre and now stopped in front of it almost motionless. As if it were the awaited signal, two women moved forward from the group of singers behind the drummers and took the cover from the object in the centre. There was an audible gasp from the crowd. It was amazing.

Custos could scarcely believe his eyes and moved closer to get a better view. Sure enough, it was a miniature replica of his house with a doll, dress and all, unmistakably like his wife, on the verandah. Two men from the group moved forward now and helped the boy to place the house on his head, and the dancing resumed. His balance was truly remarkable. On and on he danced not holding the miniature house resting on his head. Turning and leaping, gyrating now on one foot, now on both, the drummers and the singers urging him, following him, until he stood rigid in the middle of the circle, his whole body trembling with a violence that alarmed the onlookers. The house perfectly balanced on his head, trembled too, but with no danger of it falling. The old man beckoned to the two men who removed the house from the young man's head and as it left his head his hands went out, took the doll from the verandah. Now he held the doll aloft, still violently trembling. He began to speak, and at the first sound of his voice, the drummers and the singers stopped.

The whole crowd was silent, everyone holding his breath waiting. The boy lifted the doll with both hands over his head, hugged it to his chest, still speaking "unknown tongues" some thought. "But him voice sound like a woman." No one in the crowd understood the language he was using, no one except Custos. He was speaking French. And the voice was the voice of his wife. Not the voice of her later years but the voice of the young woman he had married nearly forty years ago when they had studied together in England. Dazed, Custos moved nearer because she was speaking to him, called him by the pet name she used for him in those days and the crowd was amazed to hear Custos and the boy, or so they thought, in conversation. Although they couldn't understand, clearly he was being instructed.

As soon as the instructions were given and Custos signalled that he fully understood, the voice ceased, the boy went limp and fell to the ground. The old man performed the ritual with the white rum and the shack-shack and the boy revived, normal again as if nothing had happened. Custos waited only long enough to see he was alright and called to his sons and two or three other men, "Come, I need your help. I know what has to be done and it will be done."

Well, whatever it was that the spirits told the boy no one really knew, but for the rest of the night and into the next day the men led by Custos cut down the two trumpet trees at the side of the house and dug out the roots. At the first one they went down to about eight feet, and Custos instructed them to stop and try the other one. And barely pausing the men went to work with a will. About six and a half feet down – there was nothing.

They had thought the boy described it exactly, and as Custos stared at it in shocked realisation, his mind raced back to the first day that he came to this place from the neighbouring parish where he was born and where he grew up. He remembered vividly the conversation with the old man he bought the property from. He had just returned from England with his new bride, and his father had agreed with him that they needed a place of their own where they could put down their roots. He had heard the property was for sale, it sounded ideal, two hundred acres with twenty chains bordering on the main road. He had, with his father's help, bought the property. That first day when he came, he decided where he would put the house and the depot for the citrus he would be growing. In later years he would convert the depot to the market and the packing house to a dry goods and hardware store.

The old man had jokingly said that he had heard from his grandmother from whom he inherited the property that something was buried on the property beneath a tree by slaves who almost two hundred years ago worked on the property; that anyone who disturbed any of the trumpet trees would be punished by sickness which would lead to certain death. Custos remembered that when his wife built the summer house two years ago, he had had to cut down a trumpet tree. It was right after that the sickness started. But he pushed it from his mind then and refused to believe the old man's story. Now he was face to face with the reality of it all and the boy's message from the spirits relayed through his wife's voice made sense, put side by side with the old man's tale of many years ago. So he had them dig at the place where he had cut down the old trumpet tree and they had only gone down a few feet and found it – a little earthenware jar as the spirits had described it.

He knew what he must do. If his wife was to live he must do what the spirits commanded. The little earthenware jar must be destroyed according to the prescribed manner advised by the spirits. He must send for the boy dancer. He didn't have to, the boy knew what was required and he was at that moment coming through the garden to the spot where they all stood over the jar. He asked for some kerosene oil, white rum and a piece of white bread. The bread he placed on the jar and the rum was sprinkled over it. He stood motionless and silent for a brief moment, then casually poured the kerosene oil over the jar, struck a match, and advised everyone to stand back as he piled a bundle of dry grass on the burning jar. A few seconds later, the jar burst open, emitting a heavy odour like nothing they had ever experienced before. It lasted only a few seconds and the grass fire died down leaving the empty pieces of the broken jar. The group stood speechless, until seconds later the old man who had accompanied the boy broke the silence.

"Everything all right now Custos, God be praised."

Before Custos could answer, the maid came running down to where they were. "Custos, Custos, come quick sir, Mistress asking for you. She revive sir, she revive, she sitting up in the chair in the room and she say she hungry and she want to talk to you. Lawd Custos, is a miracle... Mistress is going to live, she get over..."

Custos stood there for a moment not moving, too stunned to say or do anything, then suddenly broke into a run towards the house followed by his two sons and the other men who were with him.

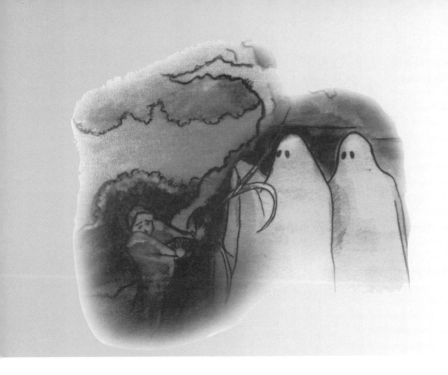

Run Big 'Fraid

Everybody knows that cotton tree is where duppies live. So everybody knew that you treat cotton tree with due respect. And whether you play or rest, or just stand up at cotton tree root to talk or laugh, you know that you are taking a chance. For if by chance you offend the spirits that inhabit that cotton tree you are likely to get in trouble, whether it's a box, in which case your face gets twisted for life, or if is a "lick" then you may get seriously ill or crippled; you might even die if your people don't know how to find the antidote for the blow. Because, according to the old people, that is how it has been from time before time.

So anybody who has any sense at all knew that there are certain things you expect when you fool round cotton tree.

But don't get me wrong you know, it is not often that the spirits will do you any harm, matter of fact, sometimes for years, for generations even, they don't bother to punish or chastise anybody for doing out of order things at the cotton tree. That's what made it so hard to know what they will do and when. It all depends on the whim and fancy of the particular duppy. So you never knew when, so you're careful all the time, so you don't get in trouble, so if it happen you have to find Baada and the Myal people to save your skin.

Well, as was said, everybody was supposed to know that. But you think some people take heed? As Miss Conse remarked, "No sir, them do them wrongs same way day after day," and because nothing happened at cotton tree for a long time, because a whole generation was growing up only hearing the stories and not really experiencing anything, some of the young people didn't believe one bit. But, as if it were her mission in life, Miss Constance was always reminding people of the happenings that she herself did not witness but of which she had heard so many stories from the older folk.

"Mi dear Miss Vie, I don't really believe in them things you know mam, I am a God fearing woman (her favourite description of herself) so I only telling you as I hear it from my great Aunt Daisy May Hutchinson of blessed memory. She say serious things gwan at that place. So I try not to pass there if I can help it but I don't really believe in it."

Cotton tree then was the meeting place, the resting place, the playroom, the everything to all the young people and some of the older folk too. Maybe that was because it was really at a convenient place in the district why it was such a popular spot. It was right in the cross roads where the two parochial roads cross and made four. So wherever you're coming from, no matter where you're going, you are bound to come to the cross roads and in so doing you are right at the cotton tree. It was the favourite meeting place for all, everybody, and meetings of one sort or another took place there. The time of day depended on who was meeting whom for what purpose. You understand.

The cotton tree grew out of a banking close to a culvert. Maybe the reason why the banking seem to get higher and higher each year is that when the men clean the road side and the culvert they pile up the sand and the fine gravel at the cotton tree root. So now the cotton tree root stood a good five feet higher than the road. Older folks remember when it was about level with the road or just a couple feet higher. But as it now stood, if you go through the culvert there was a good spot behind the banking where you could be and no one could see you or know you were there. That was the favourite hiding place for Little One. Little One was a young man about eighteen – he could be thirty, no one really knew his age. But everyone knew that he had the mind of perhaps a seven year old. Not a bright seven year old at that. Because of that everyone, especially the young men and boys, delighted in making fun of him. He was the butt of everybody's pranks and practical jokes and there were a host of stories about him and his doings. As you can guess, some of them made up by his tormentors.

He took all of this with good grace, laughing with those who laughed at the tricks they played on him. He never seemed to mind. He was kind to a fault and anything he had, his food, his money, his clothes, anyone could have for the asking. He worked with the people who owned the bakery. His job was to take the large tray loads of bread and other bake-things from the bakery to the little shops in the village and surrounding districts as many times a day as they had need to order. He kept the wooden trays spotlessly clean, as well as the bleached flour bags used to cover the bake-things he carried.

He spent every minute of his frequent free time behind the culvert at Cotton Tree where he was privy to all that went on there, and that was most of the private business of the district people. This is how corporal managed to solve plenty cases. Little One would tell him the cotton tree news and corporal just moved accordingly. Naturally he told no one of his source but his kindness and sympathy to the young man were well known.

Came the day when Little One (his real name was Constantine Hadrian Napoleon Maxifloran Thomas) got interested in a young lady. But she was not interested. How could she be interested in the acknowledged village idiot? But Little One did everything to gain her attention. Those acts were legion, and as you can imagine people made up all sorts of stories (some so ridiculous that they were not believable) about how he tried to entice the girl.

There was the story told by Lester which, according to him, he witnessed, and which earned Little One a nickname that stuck like glue. As Lester told it, he was just coming round the corner by Miss Min's shop when he saw Little One open a two-and-six bottle of Khus Khus perfume and swallow all of it. Lester said when he asked Little One the reason for such stupid action, he is reported to have said that he had visited the girl the night before and as it was pear season he broke a little wind and she complained that it smelled bad. So he drank the perfume as he was seeing her later and didn't want to run the risk for that to happen to him again. Matter of fact he was going to make sure that he did break wind but this time it would smell sweet. "No tell nobody though you know," Little One pleaded and Lester assured him he'd keep the secret. But Lester related the story at every opportunity he got to the great amusement of his friends and as the story went the rounds, Little One was renamed Sweet Breeze.

Poor fellow, he couldn't understand why all of a sudden he was being called Sweet Breeze, until one day Miss Constance asked him if it was true that he drank the perfume. Well he knew that it was only Lester who had seen him and he had promised not to tell anyone. Since the story was out, Lester had clearly betrayed him and for the first time Little One was angry and he vowed to get even with Lester. Lester was a Judas, Little One decided, but he remained as friendly as ever, so Lester never suspected that under that usual grin was the resolve to take revenge for his spreading the story. Little One bided his time till one day while he was at Cotton Tree he heard Lester and Carlton planning to frighten Old Lennon whom they overheard making a plan to meet Miss Keturiah's daughter, Dina, at the cotton tree that night. Old Lennon was known for his preference for "Young Veal" as he put it, and tried his best to bed them all. The story is that all the advances were in vain as none of them even thought of his requests seriously.

But he persisted and none escaped his attention. Carlton and Lester primed Dina and she became a part of the scheme and agreed to meet Old Lennon. The plan was she would meet him around midnight as she had to wait till her mother had gone to sleep.

Old master was delighted. At last he was going to have his longed for "Young Veal". He couldn't wait. All this plotting and counter plotting Little One heard from his hiding place and decided this was the day of his revenge. Lester's plan was that he and Carlton would get two white sheets, play duppy and frighten Old Lennon. Dina was supposed to entice him to sit on the culvert, then they would jump up from behind and frighten them.

Little One too, needed a white sheet for his plan but he had none. He was on his way to Aunt Zella to borrow a sheet when, as luck would have it, he was passing Miss Felix's house and to his joy and delight there was a white double bed sheet hanging on the line along with the other washing. He managed to get the sheet off the line without being seen. Hurrying to Cotton Tree, he promised himself that he would return the sheet before the owner missed it. He settled down in his familiar spot behind the culvert and made himself comfortable, taking care that he could not be seen. As he waited and the hours went by, various people passed. Nothing too startling happened. At last, the time approached and he heard Lester and Carlton arrive, whispering their last minute plans. Lester said, "I will take him from the right side and you from the left, remember now, don't make the sheet drop off you head."

Carlton said, "All right man everything all right. Bwoy but the mosquito dem killing me," he said slapping his right hand with the left.

It wasn't long before they heard Old Lennon coming up the road humming to himself. By arrangement, Dina appeared from the opposite side and called whispering, "Is you dat Missa Lennon?"

"Yes mi dear, me same one."

She approached him. "I thought you would never come."

"Oh no mi candy bump, nothing coulda stop me. I did think you was going to disappoint me like all the rest."

"Den you have plenty girl fren?"

"Oh no mi darling dearest, you is the only one. You know how long I wanted to ahm...ahm..." He tried to kiss her on her neck.

"What you mean?"

"Well you know what a mean."

"Meck us sit here on the culvert and tell me what you mean."

Old Lennon followed her like a puppy-dog and sat down on the concrete. "Come sit on mi lap mi turtle dove, mi heart incline."

Dina sat on his lap. "I think a too heavy for you."

"No my sweet honey cake, these legs are still strong."

Dina put her arm around his neck and said in a sultry voice, "Den you love me Missa Lennon?"

"Oh yes my precious jewel, I love you. Every part of you."

With that, his hands were on her knees and moving up her leg. At that moment, Lester and Carlton jumped from behind the culvert and Mr. Lennon jumped up pushing Dina to the ground.

"Oh my dearest God!"

His voice was full of fear. Dina screamed, Lennon turned this way, now that, confused, muttering the twenty-third psalm. Dina got up from the ground and got out of the way to allow the two duppies to do their work. They backed up Lennon who managed to start scrambling up the banking. He slipped and fell and the duppies hovered above him. He thought that was the end.

"Sweet Jesus", he mumbled but they didn't touch him as he got up and once more tried to get up the bankside. Carlton was ahead of him as he scrambled up, menacing him.

Getting a little carried away, he leaped in the air and a shrub caught the sheet exposing his legs. Lennon now realised that this was a fake and that these were not real duppies. He was just about to expose them when he saw a third duppy coming from behind the cotton tree. He surmised what was happening. Carlton and Lester saw it too and decided to make a run for it – they thought it was real – but the third duppy was agile and he knew the banking well. He kept the other two going in a tight circle, round and round. Dina took off down the road leaving her two fake duppy friends being chased by another whom they thought was real. It was a sight to see with Old Lennon enjoying the fun on the banking shouting, "Run big 'fraid, little 'fraid dey backa you, run big 'fraid, little 'fraid dey backa you." It became almost a chant. The old man was laughing and he was almost choking with delight. "No young veal coulda sweet so. Run big 'fraid, little 'fraid dey backa you..."

Well, later, when the story came out, as all stories eventually did, Lester found out that it was Little One who had put him to flight – he and Carlton and Dina. The story occupied his friends for weeks afterwards, was told and retold on the same culvert, in the bar, at the shop, everywhere. Lester and Carlton were now getting several doses of their own medicine. To crown it all, Lester was named Big 'Fraid and Carlton became known as Little 'Fraid. And Little One who was enjoying his moment of sweet revenge was no more called Sweet Breeze. To his utter delight, from that time till the day he died his name was Duppy Conqueror, a name he relished. He had at last come into his own. And you know something, people stop teasing him and making jokes at him. He was like a new person.

The Day Parson Cried

He was not a big man. Perhaps you'd say he was average size. He had a good looking body for his almost sixty years. And he was strong. He worked hard with a good deal of energy and he was well liked by the vast majority of the people of his church.

He had come to his present cure after serving among others a cure which was a mixture of the wealthy sophisticated socialites and the humble village people around. His present assignment was also a mixture of the wealthy and influential as well as humble villagers. He had seven churches under his charge so he had very little time for anything else.

His arrival was greeted with mixed feelings. There were those who welcomed him with open arms and minds, ready to cooperate and work with the new rector for the good of the parish. Others were not quite as generous. While not definitely hostile, they were nonetheless skeptical. Still others were downright unhappy with him for a number of reasons. One of the chief reasons, he was a single man. A few of the older spinsters were delighted at the prospects that that offered but wondered if he would turn out as did another minister in another denomination who was a real cassanova creating all sorts of rivalries and general mayhem among the ladies.

As usual, chief among the dissatisfied was Miss Constance. She was sure that some disaster was about to befall the Anglican Church. "After all," she asserted, "we have never had a bachelor parson in this church yet. What sort of man was all of sixty years old and don't married, don't even have and, by all account, never had a lady friend. It not natural Miss Vie. If him was a foreigner it wouldn't be so bad but he is a Jamaican."

Miss Vie didn't see what that had to do with anything. "But Miss Conse, that don't really matter," she said, "after all there is so much work that he wouldn't have time to take care of his wife."

"But she could help him." Miss Conse was now beginning to pontificate as she is accustomed to doing when she thought she had a good point, which was most of the time. "I don't like it at all Miss Vie, you know all the things that people will say, he should be a man with a wife to help him."

Well, all that was said by the people who shared Miss Conse's views didn't amount to much, for the installation of the new rector of the Anglican Church took place as scheduled, and in the welcoming speech at the ceremony Maas Charley promised the full cooperation of all concerned. And as he was not a man to mince matters or beat around the bush, he advised those who didn't mean to cooperate with the new rector to keep their mouths shut, for he reminded them, "The Lord says if you are not with me you are against me." Needless to say, that firmly established him in the minds of all as being very much in favour of the new rector. But if you knew Maas Charley well enough you would understand that he was a man of very strong views, honest to a fault in word and deed, putting up with no nonsense whatsoever from any quarter, high or low. He was known to have told the custos in no uncertain terms where to get off because Custos had dared to show his racial prejudice to a group of school children, mostly black. So, even though Maas Charley was a firm supporter of the new parson and all that was in the best interest of the church, Parson knew that if he ran afoul of him, Maas Charley would come down on him just as hard and quite as fearless.

Parson moved into the newly renovated rectory with his books, his sister who was a few years older than he was, and with a retinue of thirty-six cats and forty-two dogs. The whole village was amazed.

"Forty-two dogs, Miss Conse?" asked Aunt Julia in astonishment.

"Yes mam, and thirty-six puss," Miss Conse said and hastened to add, "I wouldn't lie to you mam."

"Oh," said Aunt Julia, "how will he ever manage to provide enough food for all those animals? You know I have a few sen-say fowls and that white Leghorn rooster that Mrs. Coley was kind enough to lend me and it is such a difficulty getting enough to feed them. I congratulate him for taking care of so many animals."

Miss Conse was not impressed. "Quite so mam," she said, "but I hear him treat the puss and the dog them better than him treat his owna sister."

As usual, Miss Conse was hearing all the stories and was adding and embellishing as it suited her, even to the point where the embellishment just wiped out any semblance of truth. But she did not care one bit, for she was one lady who didn't like the bachelor parson.

Parson knew that many people didn't like his dogs but they were his children, his friends. Mr. Rhoden was concerned that the dogs would harm the school children since the rectory was so near the school. But strangely enough this did not happen, either because the children would not venture near the rectory or because the dogs were kept confined inside the house and followed parson wherever he went. One of the favourite pastimes of the bigger boys was hiding behind one of the big poinciana trees in a position where the staircase leading up to Parson's study and bedroom was in full view, waiting till the housekeeper Miss Gatta rang the bell for lunch and then watching as the stream of dogs and cats raced down to the dining room in what seemed like an endless line. Oftentimes they would try to count them, but it was impossible and the tally varied from day to day, from checker to checker.

"Boy a ninety-two a dem me see."

"Is over a hundred me count yesterday."

"Last week I swear it was 'bout a tousan a dem."

There was no doubt Parson loved his dogs and his cats. And Parson loved his sister too and the coachman and his children. And it was a sad day when he had to bury his sister who had not been at all well. In fact, the story is that she had never been a well person from childhood. Occasionally too, when he had to bury a dog or a cat, he was exceptionally sad.

But perhaps the animal he loved the best out of the lot was his horse. He had no motor car. Cars were rare in those days and rarer still during the war. So Parson had to rely on his faithful horse, Doris, his buggy and his coachman to take him around to the various churches on his duties. And the faithful Doris never let him down. For years she was a most reliable performer and in rain and sunshine, night or day, long or short journeys, Doris took her master wherever he needed to be. She performed so well that the coachman affectionately called her Lady Doris.

One day, coming down from Niagra, the coachman noticed that she had a slight limp on her right hind leg. He mentioned it to Parson as he stopped, examined the leg, thinking that she had picked up a gravel but there was none in her hoof. He could see nothing wrong so they continued the journey. The limp was less visible as they got on the main road which was paved but he decided to watch it. A few days later he noticed the limp again and as the days progressed it got worse, so bad she couldn't walk. Lady Doris was tied out on the cricket field adjoining the rectory grounds and Maas Charley lent Parson a horse for the time being.

The vet came and advised that she had strained a ligament. It would take some time but she should be well again and as good as new. But that did not happen, and several months later, after all that was possible had been done for Lady Doris, Parson had to take the decision that she was to be put to sleep. The coachman was sent to ask the corporal in charge of the police station if he would kindly come and put the animal out of its misery. He said he would and he could come at midday the following day. It was indeed a sad time for Parson and the coachman.

Early that morning, some men began digging a hole in which the animal would be buried. By about eleven o'clock they were ready and the coachman led Lady Doris from the stable to the spot. It took a long time, the old girl could barely walk and she was clearly in pain. A few people had gathered, some school boys among them. Parson came out of the rectory as soon as Corporal was steering his bicycle through the school gate. Poor Parson, it was clear that this was a difficult time for him, his eyes were red and watery. No one spoke. Corporal took out his service revolver and told everyone to stand back.

Everyone moved to a safe distance and, satisfied that they were out of harm's way, Corporal raised the weapon to the level of Lady Doris' head which was bowed low. There was a click as the safety catch was released and as Corporal was about to fire, Parson in a voice charged with grief, said, "Just a minute." Corporal lowered his arm and Parson rushed to the head of the animal. Lady Doris in a supreme effort lifted her head as she felt Parson's arm around her neck. He hugged and patted her, tears streaming down his face contorted with grief. The coachman too was quietly weeping. "Goodbye old girl, and thank you." He was weeping now, his big shoulders shaking visibly. The boys who had never thought that they would ever see Parson cry, looked at each other in astonishment but no one laughed. Moments later he let go of Lady Doris' head and ran towards the rectory.

Corporal waited till he was well inside the building and once more raised the revolver.

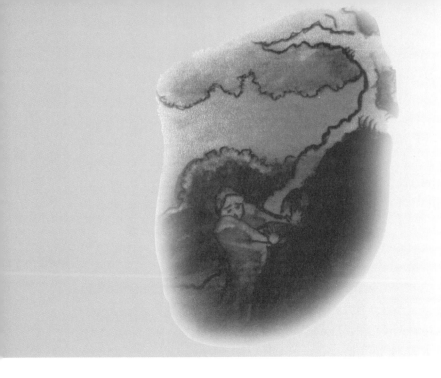

Whooping Boy

It was Christmas time again. The season came as it did last year and the year before last year and the year before that, for generations, as long as anybody could remember, as always heralded by bitter-bush blossom and yellow Christmas rose which was not a rose at all but a wild flower from the chrysanthemum family growing on the bank sides, lush and green and blooming in profusion at Christmas time. This bright yellow, almost gold flower, was joined by other yellow bloomers, wild nickal, black eye Susan, ram-goat-dashalong, Jerusalem candlestick, the tall majestic karato on the hillsides and all manner of yellow blooming plants, shrubs and vines.

Miss Conse observing this each year was often heard to remark, "Jamaica Christmas yellow fi true."

As far as you could see there were wild yellow flowers of all sizes and shapes blooming everywhere, and the white bitter-bush powder-puff-looking blooms smelling so sweet, perfuming the air for good distances around. As soon as these appeared, we children would run on the open commons shouting and chanting, "Bitter bush a blaasam, Chrismus a come."

Then the "most-Chrismus" activities began with the action and the excitement growing with each day leading up to the big day. The Sunday school children's rehearsal of the Nativity scene, the familiar carols with one or two new ones and the recitations and skits got more intense and urgent, stressing out the teachers and the organist.

At home, the preparations and the excitement were no less. The Christmas hog would be slaughtered, the pork corned and smoked and some adventurous ladies would attempt to make their own hams. They had learned from the Welfare Lady when they attended a training day and were taught how to treat the pork legs. Needless to say there were varying degrees of success, but no matter the outcome they all could boast a homemade ham for Christmas. The men, not to be left out, dug the yams, white and yellow, sweet-yam and the gummy mozella. These be cured and prepared for market or home use. Those who liked rum punch would make their special brew and specially stored them to ripen as they would do the sorrel and the ginger beer, all carefully timed to coincide with the special days of the season. One way of curing these brews was to bury the containers in the ground for a few weeks.

The special entertainment would also start. The Village music band would play on selected week nights in Uncle

Sam's tailor shop and some young and not so young persons, chiefly men, would gather and dance on the little grass lawn beside the shop. On weekends, Friday and Saturday nights, the band moved to Mr. Wong's shop piazza where the crowd would gather and where the dancing would continue under the light of the bright Tilly gas lamp the cunning shopkeeper would hang in the window. He knew the more people gathering, the more his goods would sell, especially liquor. As usual, he had brought in special stock for the holiday celebrations. Extra liquor, aerated waters assorted, special sweet biscuits, some in special tins. Crepe paper and tinsel ribbon, lots of baubles, and for the children, special toys and the balloons and the fee-fees and the clappers that children have to have because these things said it was Christmas, and they couldn't imagine Christmas without them. There were those adults too who couldn't imagine Christmas without the green gungo peas, and they would search far and near for this traditional and precious addition to the Christmas dinner, paying the inflated price of the season. That is, of course, if they hadn't managed to plant their own in April.

The ladies too would have put their fruits, currants, raisins and prunes, to soak in rum and cheap wine even from then so it would be ready for the baking of all the Christmas cakes and puddings. On baking days, they would gather in various groups at Miss Allene, at the community oven and the whole village would be reeking with the smell of the delicious fruit-cakes they were making. Apart from the cakes there would be puddings and pones of all sorts, cassava, cornmeal, sweet potato, all part of the season's tradition.

The commercial bakeries would make special duck bread and crown bread. Undoubtedly, Christmas was the season everyone, young and old alike, looked forward to with eager anticipation. And it was the only season when children were allowed to eat as much as they liked or as

much as they could hold. Bottled drinks which were rarely had over the year, except on special occasions like birthdays, were generously given and it was the only time when each child would be given a whole bottle for him or herself. That was heaven. And each one hoarded their precious drinks, thinking the fizz would last, much to their disappointment, for as soon as the bottle was opened and the first sips taken the fizz was gone, leaving flavoured sugar and water which was sipped as if it were the rarest wine.

Parents begged children to "eat up" and they did justice to the occasion, some overdoing it. But whether or not, there was the washout to face at the end of the season. Those were the generous doses of castor oil to cleanse the system of all the extras consumed. We hated it but there was no escape. It was part to the tradition.

Nearer the day, like the week before, John Canoe bands would begin to roam the streets, and on weekend nights would end up at Mr. Wong's shop where the light was. Each time someone made a donation, especially a silver coin, the dancing would intensify, sometimes getting quite bawdy and suggestive so we children would be forbidden to watch. But we watched anyhow, and in secret imitated the antics and the movements of the characters like Devil, Horsehead, Cowhead, Bellywoman, Doctor, Pitchy Patchy, and the favourite Actor Boy with the beautifully decorated miniature house, if the band could afford it, would make its appearance on Christmas Eve.

While this was going on, we children and all who would listen would be regaled with stories about Christmas from the Bible and also from the older folks' memory bank. There were duppy stories too, some of them detailing their antics at Christmas-time so scary, some children would go to bed many nights in fear with the cover over their heads.

One of the favourite Christmas stories, more for the teller than the listener, was the story of the Whooping Boys. These were supposed to be the ghosts of the young boys and young men as well, whose job it was in slavery time, to drive the cattle from pasture to pasture, from pasture to the pens. A lot more of this activity took place at Christmas time, especially on Christmas Eve, because work ceased for the two days holiday and the animals had to be secured. These fellows, to make their work lighter, would use the time to whoop and call out to the cattle, singing their made up songs. These songs would be topical, about things and happenings on the particular estate. This whooping and singing earned them the name.

The chief Whooping Boy story came from a young man who worked at the sugar factory and whose job it was to move the cattle about on the instructions of Busha, so he knew all about cattle, particularly estate cattle, which was needed to draw ploughs and cane carts and the drays. He was a member of a group that called themselves the Scouts – not to be confused with the Boy Scouts – who marched and sang, in uniform, on special occasions, to the music of fife and drum. He had many fantastic tales of his own encounters with these ghost boys whom he described as his friends and kindred spirits since he was doing the same job that they had done.

"One night ah was comin from the factory and it was late late, me alone on the dark dark road. As a reach by the bamboo lane I hear dem comin up Spring Hill. Ah hide myself in a bamboo clump waiting to see dem come over the brow of the hill. Ah hear dem comin and the whooping and the calling and di singing getting louder and louder as dem come nearer an a so dem a sing an call, so dem a fire dem whip...Woop woop, Back cow, back cow, Ayee, Oh haa, Oh haa...di whip dem a fire pye pye. I hear dem plain as day singing 'Busha a sleep in a Missis bed, mi haffi sleep pon banana trash, mi one mi one – pye pye, Busha a sleep and snore loud loud, mi haffi wuck till mi drop dung dead, dead dead, pye pye'."

He sang his heart out, imitating the sound of the whooping and the whip. "Whoop whoop, back cow, back cow, pye pye, and a wait an wait, so dem whoop so dem flash dem whip and the soun come near and a swear any second ah woulda see dem comin over the hill. Den all of a sudden the noise stop and it was quiet quiet for a short time, then when it start again, this time it was on the opposite side like dem pass mi and di soun now coming from up by the church."

The story ended, "Ah neva see dem dat night, but mi uncle sey him si dem one long time when im was a boy a go a school. An im tell mi wha fi do fi mek mi si dem."

Try as we and all his listeners might we did not see the Whooping Boys, not that or later Christmases when we kept watch. We never even heard the whooping. We couldn't find anyone else who had seen or heard them or any of the other famous reported manifestations like Three-foot horse and River Mumma.

The stories and their telling were highly amusing and intriguing and we were on the verge of believing when one Christmas we had the shock of our lives. Our story teller told us that he was walking on the road and he heard the boys coming, but this time, acting on his uncle's instructions, he saw them. Not only did he see them, he walked with them and heard them talking about the next time they would appear and where and when. He would take us to the spot if we all paid him. So eager were we to see these ghosts we agreed, handed over our precious threepence pieces, all six of us, and agreed to meet at twelve o'clock the next night at the culvert near the cross roads leading to the factory. We were to hide behind the culvert and listen and wait for the whooping boys to make their appearance. We were to be sure to be there before midnight, as that was the time they would come. We were warned to make no sound or movement whatsoever or tell anyone, not even "yu Modder" a word about it.

We spent the whole day scheming how we were to get out of our homes at that hour, but we were able to sneak out without detection and we all assembled as agreed. We hid behind the culvert and waited. It must have been midnight when, sure enough, we heard a whooping and a cracking of a whip. It went on for a few minutes. We got very excited and none of us noticed how similar the voice we were hearing was to our storyteller's, and that there was only one voice. Neither did we notice that he was nowhere in sight. The sound suddenly ceased, and when it started again it was coming from the opposite direction, just as he had described it, it seemed to have passed us unnoticed. Then the sound stopped again and while we were wondering at the happening, there was our storyteller coming from up the hill. Panting and quite breathless he tried to explain that he saw them coming and seeing him, they started to chase him so he had to run or they would have caught him and perhaps harmed him. He insisted that one of us must have moved or spoken, that's why they disappeared.

While he was there telling us how he had heard, seen, and outrun the Whooping boy, Corporal arrived on his bicycle.

"Come here young man," Corporal said, and he obeyed.

"You are up to yu ole tricks again. You think I don't know that is yu mecking all that noise and trying to fool these children about that Whooping boy foolishness. I have a good mine lock yu up for public mischief."

He realized that Corporal was on to his ruse and admitted that he was trying to scare us but it was all a joke. He confessed that he was calling all the way up the hill and when he reached teacher's gate, he ran through the bushes to the train line, followed the line past us, called from that side, and then ran back to approach from the side from which we first heard the sound. No wonder he was puffing and blowing like the old train engine.

He begged Corporal to give him a chance as he meant no harm, only to frighten us a little. "Is jus a likkle joke Sir Corpral."

"What is joke to you is death to bullfrog."

He was set free with a warning, "Don't let me ever see you doing that or any of yu tricks again, yu lucky is Christmas, gwan yu ways and see that these boys get home safe."

But we would not let him get away so freely, just so. We demanded and got back our money to start with and we gave him a nickname that was to remain with him for years until long after we had all grown up. He was known thereafter as "Chrismus Cowboy".

That was the last we heard about Whooping Boy except from Miss Conse who said, "An yu know when me was a little girl my Granny tell mi say she know people who use to hear them every Christmas Eve. But mi no know. Pity she dead an gone now."

Who Dat?

The full moon had risen well over Spring Hill, lighting the road leading up to Crossing. In the quiet of the cool night, the sound of crickets and toads was accompanied by Simon and Johnny, strumming on the old banjo cut from the root of an old cedar tree, singing their latest composition, enjoying the music and the story the song told. This new ballad gave them no end of amusement as did the many others before, more so because of who they thought was involved.

It was the custom that events, be they sad or happy, that happened or were rumoured, were "put into song". Sometimes real names were used, sometimes titles, but most times the names were disguised but so cleverly that even

170

without calling names you could tell who exactly was the target. So when the boys sang, "Green bush, green bush, mine wasp sting yu", everyone knew that the song referred to the beating that Miss Pearlie, the brown skin lady, gave to her rival, leaving her with a swollen face that closed her eyes for days. You see, whenever you got stung by a wasp in your face the saying was that "Brown gal kiss yu" and the incantation when you were approached by a wasp was "Green bush, green bush". Then there was the story of the train driver and the fireman who were along with the same lady and when the three were supposed to have been seen together in the most unusual, compromising position, the boys sang "Train a blow, yu nuh hear the train a blow, di driver pon top and fireman below, hear di train a blow". "Whai Maybell drop inna hole" told the story of the young girl who, one dark night, fell into the partially dug toilet pit.

So this night was no different. The latest rumour concerned the young Parson from the old church on the hill. The story was he was seen at the bamboo patch, late one night with a young woman. This spot was famous as a meeting place for lovers as it was off the main road hidden by clumps of bamboo. The fact that his young wife was away with her parents for the last few weeks recuperating after giving birth to their first child was the fuel the rumour needed to spread. The young Parson was bound to be "under pressure". It was now almost a month since he was without his wife. Some idle boys, including Paulie and Thomas, returning from a "set up" late the Friday night saw two persons they said were naked lying down on the soft fallen bamboo leaves. Instead of going about their business, these idlers said they called out, only to see them run, clothes in hand, into the thick bush nearby. So sure they were of who they saw, the next day the song was out.

"Who dat a ly dung deh...Parson... eena di bamboo nuh Parson". The boys sang this with great amusement, and soon most people in the village were also singing this latest ballad.

Miss Conse who did not pay these songs much mind, strangely enough, was among those singing this, although privately. For a few days, she enjoyed the fun. This was for two reasons. The young Parson was not one of her favourite persons. According to her, he had ignored her at church one Sunday, and Miss Conse was someone you ignored at your peril. And she added to that, the song was sweet.

"Well mam," she confided to Miss Vie, "to think of it, what a disgrace"

"Yu caant listen to all those idle people a say ," Miss Vie said.

" Well ole time people say when yu hear a story, if a nuh even so, is nearly so it goh. There must be some amount of trute in di story." Miss Conse was sure.

The story had been going the rounds for a few days and everybody was so caught up in the excitement that no one really gave a thought to the "facts" as were told or even bothered to find out the facts and as you can guess everyone had his or her own version. It was Aunt Julia, with her always skeptical mind, who first really questioned the story. You see, Aunt Julia was the wife of Uncle Ben, who for years sat as a juror on many important cases in the Parish. She was accustomed to listening to him reasoning out the arguments as presented in court as he sat in the corner of the verandah talking to himself, and many times this art of reasoning she transferred to happenings and stories and rumours, quite often with very good results, earning her the reputation of being a wise old lady.

"But Miss Conse, think about it," she said "you think im would do something like dat, a man in his position?"

"It look doubtful, but man is man, an yu never know who to trus." Miss Conse still held on to the story.

"Well I have mi doubts for the story not straight, an if how I hear it, is so it really go, it don't make sense to me at all and it could be anybody else," Aunt Julia continued.

"Well dem say di bwoy dem see im as plain as day, inna di white shirt im always wearin, doh dem never see im face."

"Stop right there Miss Conse," said Aunt Julia. "The story I hear is that dem was naked. So im didn't have on any shirt, an in the shadow of the bamboo yu really couldn't tell who was who, it could be anybody and everybody know say Paulie an Thomas a two liard. Dem lie like a horse a gellop a race course."

"Is true yu know, Aunt Julia, an a Friday night dem say it happen, but come to think of it, a Saturday evening mi meet Parson a Crossing a come offa di evening train, say im was at Synod in Spanish Town, so im wasn't even here Friday night, so it couldn't bi him."

"See what a tell yu, it not good to listen to rumour and story, and much more to spread them. Look how people bad talking the poor young man an giving him bad name wid dem lie and story, even a put him eena song, the poor innocent man."

"True true Aunt Julia, me a go broadcast it and meck sure everybody know say a couldn't be him for me see im a come offa train Saturday, an mi have witness for im stop an talk to me an Miss Agnes an Miss Bee. Look how dem wicked eeh mam?"

Knowing her, it wouldn't take her more than a day to spread the true story. "That is the best thing you can do, after all, you help spread the rumour too."

"An wi coulda get wiself into trouble...but all the same di song sweet mi."

Cotton Tree Blues

Morning breaks at cotton tree
Set in the middle of the village cross roads
And the parade begins to pass before sunrise
Here their life is exposed, on show
At this most famous spot
Market women with their loads
Wait for their truck
Farmers go on their way to field and "grung"
Children pass on their sometimes reluctant way
To teacher school and class
People on their way to post office shop and clinic
Well into noon afternoon and evening
And when it would seem to stop
Young lovers meet in the dark
To the call of a young night hawk
Then all is quiet and still
Friendly ghosts gleefully frolic
On their way to the church yard on the hill
Playfully scaring those brave enough to be out
Cotton tree Cotton tree
The stage on which the village life-drama
We see played and replayed and played again
For decades and decades
Far more than three score years and ten.

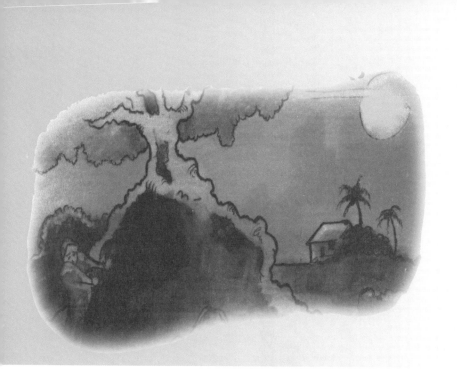

Reaction Time

The whole village from corner to corner was buzzing with the good news. Miss Clemmy one-son Phillip win a big scholarship to go to high school. He was known to be the brightest boy in the whole elementary school, everybody knew that, and because he was so bright and gifted, teacher confidently entered him for the scholarship. To ensure that the form reached the right office in time, teacher delivered it himself one day when he went into Kingston. From the entry form went in, teacher spent most evenings and weekends too drilling the boy in his lessons, preparing him for the examination.

The Sunday before the date, the whole church prayed that God would bless him with success. Many persons also

told the young man and his mother that they were praying for him.

When the results were announced a few months later, the whole village received the news with great joy. Phillip had won a full scholarship to a very prestigious High School. "Full scholarship Miss Vie, that mean everything provide. Book, school fee, boarding, uniform and pocket money yu know. Yu know what dat mean fi poor Clemmy, an she struggle so hard. All di same mi not surprise. Im bright caan't done. An di most importantis ting, every Sunday im in church wid im modder. Him is God bless. To God be the Glory." Miss Conse too, like everybody else, was celebrating.

Indeed he was blessed, for it was not easy to get into that school, or any high school for that matter. There were a limited number of places in the schools, especially the better ones, and your pocket had to be deep and well lined. To get a full scholarship was something else, again these were very rare indeed. High school was, for the majority of youngsters, just a dream.

To say the whole village was celebrating, was to put it mildly. Everywhere the young man went people crowded around him, congratulated him, making it quite clear that they were all proud of him. Some persons even said as much. Their pride was boundless. Old Lennon, seeing Phillip at the shop said, "Come here boy, I hear good things about you...good going mi bwoy." At that, he put a five shilling note in Phillip's hand. "Little something, I was going to buy a drink, but I can do without that today." That was no ordinary thing, for Old Lennon was known for his love of the bottle.

Other persons were equally generous. Maas Benjy, the railway man, gave him a brand new two and sixpence piece, and Uncle Fuddy gave him a pretty ewe kid. Everybody you could think of was glad. Those who had nothing to give, showered him with love and good wishes and were proud and happy at his success. Miss Clemmy too came in for her fair share of praise and plaudits from all.

That was everybody except Mammy Baker whose heart seemed to be full of envy and spite, and empty of all love and compassion. She had no joy in the prosperity of others, especially young men, for she had some weird idea that they were in competition with her two teenaged boys. They were not doing well in school, were often absent and were known to be lazy. Teacher had to speak to them and their mother quite frequently about their approach to their schoolwork. He pointed out to their mother that if only the boys would apply themselves they could be so much better. Frequently they said, they had to help their mother on the little holding to plant and weed and reap. This was clearly an excuse, as the little place did not need all that they pretended to be doing. Their mother upheld them in all of this, and even made it known that as far as school was concerned that was not all that necessary, as the balm yard Mother had assured her that the oil she gave her would do the work. So they were all about in their idleness, making all kinds of little trouble.

And yet she thought that they were so innocent, well behaved young people and made all kinds of excuses for their bad behaviour and bad manners sometimes. This annoyed and upset Miss Conse. "She tink dem is so wonderful an caan't mash ants. Ah no lie dem say every Jackass tink dem pickney a race horse, an every Jangkro tink dem pickney white."

"Well Miss Conse, you always have a plaster fi every sore," Miss Vie remarked.

"An it no stop dey so Miss Vie, she no like fi see odder people pickney prosper yu know, she is a wicked woman. I even hear say iniquity involve."

The talk was that Mammy Baker had said that people had worked on her two boys and try to "tun dem dung" and so she made several trips with them to different balm yards and spent good monies on guard rings and other "protection". It was said also that she in turn tried to work on people she did not like, even for no good reason, and on those she envied, to make sure that they would not succeed.

"Mi dear Miss Vie, yu si how Earnest stay? Mi hear say from di day she borrow Earnest pen a post office, the bright bwoy tun fool an im finga dem cramp up and im can't write again...im stap learn an seem de now, a walk a road and a pick leaf. Clean out a im hed, mi hear say a she dweet, but Gawd naw sleep."

"I hear those stories, but Miss Conse I don't believe in dem things, no mam not me," Miss Vie said emphatically shaking her head.

"Well mam, evil in di worl, an her owna sister say it, it not no secret dats why di sister stop talk to her and she no go a har yard none tall. But one day, one day she gwine pay."

But Mammy Baker paid no heed to all the talk. She made her usual frequent trips to obeah man after obeah man with a few obeah women in between, seeking help. Sometimes these journeys took her all over the island, up mountain, down valleys and by seaside. As the story goes, she was going to make sure that the bright boy Phillip, everybody's pet, turn worthless. Neither Phillip nor his mother had done anything to hurt her or her sons and they paid no mind to the talk that he, Philip, was being "worked on".

Phillip had gone off to school as planned, and as the years passed he excelled at his studies, and to everyone's delight he got another scholarship to go to England to study medicine. Mammy Baker thought that that was the limit and intensified her evil activities all to no avail, for Phillip also excelled in England, graduated with honours, was also awarded a grant for post graduate work, and in a short while was recognized by his University in England as one of their top graduates, as his research work in the treatment of heart diseases was acclaimed world wide. So Phillip prospered, so Mammy Baker's two sons, now grown men, sunk deeper and deeper into drunkenness and sloth, into utter uselessness, scorned by the villagers.

"A reaction Miss Vie," said Miss Conse, "but yu don't si the end yet, the last stage of a man or woman is worse dan di firs."

Then one of Mammy's sons died suddenly and they thought mysteriously, except Miss Conse who predicted correctly what the post mortem would reveal. "Is either rum or reaction." The doctor agreed. He had died from an excess of alcohol in his blood, coupled with malnutrition and a possible heart condition. Mammy took it to heart, and not long after, less than a year, the other son followed. He fell out of a breadfruit tree which he had foolishly climbed when he was half-drunk. A broken spine, the Doctor said.

This totally devastated the old lady. No amount of support and compassion she received from the village people helped. Undeserving as she was, people were in sympathy and rallied to her side. Few weeks after the death of her second son, she took to bed ill. She had no obvious physical ailment the doctor could detect. She was not that old. It was more in her mind, he said. True, there was no physical pain that she felt, but she seemed tormented.

The Doctor couldn't find out why she cried and whimpered day and night, slept very little and only after he prescribed some sleeping tablets. She ate very little and this went on for some time.

Then she began to complain of feeling hot, yet when she was felt for fever she was cool and normal. She, however, continued to mumble incoherently, not making sense. She next complained that she felt as though she was being pricked by pins and needles all over her body. She now had to be propped up in the bed as she couldn't stand or even sit in a chair. The good people of the church took turns in caring for her, as she had no one else. She had so alienated most of her friends, there was hardly anyone to come to her aid. Prayer meetings were held by the parson and some church sisters and brothers. They begged God to have mercy on her, to heal her, to relieve her of her suffering. Strangely, all they heard from her was whimpering and mumbling. She took part in none of the prayers or Psalms.

One night when they gathered around her to pray she was in almost a rage, tossing and writhing, crying, mumbling, trying to talk but no one could understand a word she was saying. This went on for a while as the praying continued. Then suddenly they heard her clearly say, "Oh God have mercy, oh God help me," then she became quiet, as though she was listening to someone or something, her eyes closed. Soon they heard her say in a whisper, "Yes Lord, yes Lord," and in a loud voice, clear and strong, they heard her confess to the evils she had done to various persons, a long and varied list including even some of those praying at her bedside, persons for whom and on whom she had worked obeah. Miss Conse whispered to Miss Vie, "Confession is good for the soul." Everyone was astounded as she ended, "Please Massa Gad, forgive me, forgive me, forgive me Lord Gad and Jesas forgive, forgive." Her voice faded to a whisper and then into silence. She was still and quiet as a sleeping baby.

The brethren led by Parson continued their praying for a few more minutes and someone raised the hymn "It is well with my soul". At the end of the singing they thought she was asleep, but she had died quietly, peacefully as they prayed.

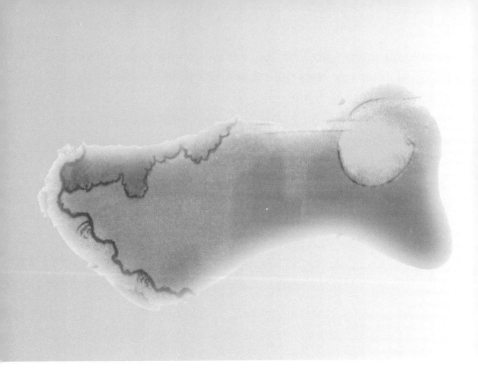

Love Story

The afternoon sun beat down fiercely on the dusty, lonely country road. There was no vehicular traffic in sight except the Royal Mail van which went spluttering and puffing up the steep incline of "quarter-mile hill", at the top of which were the village shops, the post office, the police station, the school, the Anglican Church, the tailor-shop and the railway crossing.

The two riders, each on a saddled mule, came to a stop under the spreading welcome shade of the old guango tree at the foot of the hill. It was customary for riders and "walk-foot" travellers to pause here, rest awhile, and sometimes water their animals – in the old cistern left there by the property owners for just that purpose – before starting their

journey up to the village square. They had, many years ago, named the place Jacob's Well. Jacob was the name of the son of the old property owner's son.

Maas Henry, the Chinese shopkeeper who had the largest shop in the village, and his long time friend Maas Aleck, the carpenter and builder, had ridden six miles to Prospect and back to look at the shop building that Maas Henry was thinking of acquiring for his only son Alton, now twenty-one. Even though Alton was his chief assistant with the shop and the small bakery, Maas Henry felt it was time he went out on his own, start a family and run his own life independently. And judging by the many young ladies in and around who seemed to fancy him, he would certainly have the pick of the bunch.

He was a handsome young man, well-built, with an open, laughing face and pleasing personality. He seemed to have inherited the best of both worlds – his father's good looks and pleasant demeanor and the strong body of his tall black mother whose relatives were known to be the tallest and the strongest in the area. Alton himself was over six feet tall and was the apple of his father's eye. Having completed high school with distinction, he was bright and promising. He was a very eligible young man. Their business was prosperous and growing. They were people of some means. He was truly a good catch for any decent, ambitious young woman, according to several older ladies and gentlemen.

As they rested under noon day shade, Maas Henry asked his friend, "Maas Aleck, what you think...good spot?" It was usual for him to ask Maas Alex's advice on such matters relating to buildings and locations. He respected his friend's opinion.

Maas Alex agreed. "And the building is a substantial one...cut stone and it have a good roof...four rooms upstairs and bathroom, two rooms downstairs at the back, good kitchen, and there is plenty land to expand later."

"The price good to," Maas Henry said, pleased with himself.

"After you is such a good bargainer, you bargain hard with the old lady," Mass Alex said with an admiring smile.

"She anxious to sell, me see dat. Me decide to buy. Sunday me carry the money to make down payment. You come with me.

"Ok, Ok, me know, after Church ova...Nine a clock then?" Mass Alex agreed and mused, "I hope Alton like it though."

"Mus like. Me like. Him do what me say. Me stock it good for him. Him soon can mally now."

"Talking about that, who yu think im going married to? Im seem to like Girlie, Corporal daughter, and she certainly like him."

"No no she too maga, no good to work an have children. Me want plenty strong grandson," Maas Henry said firmly. "Maybe me sen go China for good Chiney girl, plenty girl in China want to mallied."

"But that might not suit Alton, him is like im father, im like Jamaican girl," Mass Aleck teased his friend. "What you say to that?" "That no matter ef girl decent, him can marry who ever him like, if she good woman like he madda." He was much more liberal and enlightened than his peers.

"Black girl, Chiney girl, brown girl, alla same, only mus have decent mine. Look he madda, Look Miss Caro...she good good woman know? Work hard, look after family, look after me tu, she di bes. Me mally har when she just twenty year old."

He was talking of his own wife, Miss Caroline. Everybody who knew her, respected and acknowledged her as a good woman and a real mother to all. Now in her forty-fifth year, she had earned the respect and love of everyone, and all marvelled how two persons from such differing backgrounds could come together, half-way around the world, and find happiness and love. "True," Maas Aleck said, "she in a class by herself."

No more was said. Maas Henry took out his pipe and tobacco pouch, filled his pipe, and soon the smooth nice smelling smoke he was puffing gave evidence of the fine imported tobacco he smoked, which he blended with local "Jackass rope".

They rode off up the hill and soon Maas Aleck asked, "Then when Alton gone how you gwine to manage?"

"Memba me have Harry. Mi train him good. Memba him wid mi since he come outa school. Him good hones' hard working man an him related to Miss Caro."

The rest of the way they rode in silence, up the steep hill, and finally they arrived at the shop. Percy, the handyman, took Maas Henry's mule, stripped off the saddle and turned him loose on the little common at the back of the shop. Maas Aleck dismounted and they went into the shop. Maas Henry asked, "Aleck you want drink?"

Maas Aleck accepted the usual offer of white rum and water. "Thanks".

"No forget Sunday."

He said he would remember, as Alton, who was just coming from the produce store room, greeted him. "Howdy Maas Aleck, how is everything?"

"Good mi son. Good. Yu father will tell you. But im meck a good bargain tidday. Im buyin Mother Perrin shop building. An im say is fi yu."

"Why yu bodder wid dat now Papa." He tried to disguise his pleasure.

"A soon time fi you married now," his father said, "and settle dung an stop runnin roun like ram puss." It was Maas Aleck who offered that advice.

"No Maas Aleck, I behaving myself."

"No give me dat. Ah mi yu a talk to. We all know how it go. But teck mi advice, is time yu settle dung...an yu father have a good plan fi yu to run dat shop a Prospec."

"Well that suit me," Alton said, again trying to hide his delight. "Pearlie just tell me this morning that she think she pregnant," he confided to Maas Aleck, "and we decide to talk to wi parents an set the date."

"But look mi crosses, bwoy, clear a Parson yard you go." Maas Aleck, clearly pleased, tried to hide his delight. "Well unno young people no stap yah. All di same, when mango ripe you no haffi tell it fi drop."

Needless to say, Maas Henry and Miss Caro received the news with disbelief, but they were well pleased. Pearlie was regarded as one of the finest young ladies in the village – she was the Baptist parson's niece – decent, upright, bright and good looking, taking her dark cool complexion from her Indian mother, and to top it all she was known to be a shy, sedate girl. After some discreet questioning, Miss Caro discovered that Alton was her very first real boyfriend, the first man for her. That pleased her no end. And it was she who went to Parson and his wife to explain everything and to ask their blessing. Maas Henry's only remark was, "Dat baby going be a good looking baby."

Parson and his wife gave their consent and set a date. The wedding took place as planned, quiet, not much fuss, with Miss Caro crying a little. Maas Henry, beaming, gave his new daughter, as he styled her, the Chinese traditional gifts of gold and promised that when his grandson was born – it was a boy he was sure – he would give him a big

Christening dinner and invite everybody. Maas Aleck completed the necessary repairs and adjustments and additions to the building at Prospect in record time and the week after the wedding, the young couple was duly installed in their new home, complete with the room designated, the baby's room, painted a light blue for the boy.

When the baby came it was the prettiest little girl you could ever see, with honey coloured skin and dark brown eyes. Papa Henry was disappointed; nevertheless, he showered the baby with gifts of jewelry, including a nice pair of Chinese gold bangles. Alton was proud as anything with his baby daughter. He wanted to name her Carolyn after his mother, but Papa Henry insisted that she should have a Chinese name so he named her Precious Jade, but everybody called her Little Miss Caro. And she grew pretty and sweet and was a real joy to her young parents.

Then other babies followed in rapid succession and in a matter of ten years, they had four bouncing boys one after the other, and then to end it all, another daughter, equally as pretty as the first. Maas Henry was delighted and to see him with his six grandchildren was a real treat. Frequently, he would hire Mr. Burton's car and go to Prospect for them to spend Sunday with him and their grandmother, who was equally pleased and proud. Sundays after she took them to church she spent the rest of the day playing with them, making all sorts of goodies for them, making dolly clothes and even playing cricket with the boys. Maas Henry was busy in the kitchen cooking their favourite foods, and it was always just before dark that he returned them to their grateful parents who were glad to have had the day's rest from their six active lively children.

The children were taught to call their grandparents by the Chinese endearing names. So they were known as

Goong Goong (grandfather) and Po Po (grandmother). Soon the whole village was calling them by those names.

Every one of the children was bright in school, so Maas Henry began to pick careers for them. He wanted no less than two doctors, two engineers, one accountant and one lawyer. He even dreamed that Jade would be the first woman barrister of Chinese ancestry in the country. So he schemed and planned and worked and saved the money he would need to help them achieve his goals for them. His grandchildren, born from his only child, were his life.

Alton's business prospered and he and Pearlie remained in love and the whole district of Prospect could see this love between them. He took care of his wife and she of him, their life was good. And Miss Caro's joy knew no bounds when they both decided to get confirmed in the church she attended. That was the year before the first two children would take that step. Thereafter, every year, one of the children was confirmed, except the last year when the last two were confirmed together. That year, he and Pearlie took over the Christmas treat his father was accustomed to give for the children and the aged, and as often happens in country districts, he and Pearlie were now referred to as Maas Alton and Miss Pearlie.

Maas Henry, in honour of the confirmation of his son and daughter, got Maas Aleck to repair the broken windows and broken benches in the church. On top of that, he had a big confirmation lunch for Parson, and Bishop teacher and Post Mistress, his close friends and the children's godparents. It was a grand affair.

One by one, the children grew up and left to go to High School. They all did well and before you knew it were off to College in America where they all went, except for Washington and Benjamin who decided to go to England, one to study law, the other medicine.

In the end Maas Henry got his wish. Two became doctors, one an engineer, two became lawyers – one a company lawyer. The last girl entered a Roman Catholic Convent in Kingston to become a nun, and ended up being a High School teacher. Life was good. Maas Henry loved the church and gave generously. Even though he didn't attend, he knew his beloved Caro loved her Lord and her church and that pleased him.

Alton and Pearlie were very active in the life and work of the church and earned the respect of their fellow members. Alton's business prospered. He bought a truck, then a car. He used his truck to transport market people at minimal charge, and his car was always available to take persons to the doctor twelve miles away, and only charged what could be afforded when he did charge. Many times he accepted kind for payment, sometimes it was free of cost. He had expanded his business and built a fairly large bakery when his father gave up baking. He was able to buy two new bread vans and now hired about twenty-four persons to work for him and, like his parents, he was good and generous to the poor. He was well loved.

As they were getting older, his parents gave up the business. They encouraged Harry to take over, which he did. The money for the business was to be paid in manageable installments. The building which they had owned was given to Harry gratis. They had built a lovely house about a mile away on land acquired from Miss Caro's relatives, so they could be near family, and that house soon became the centre of family comings and goings. And Maas Henry found every reason to cook up a big dinner or lunch.... Birthdays, graduations, Chinese New Year, Christmas, Easter and first of August, or just when his son and daughter or one of the grandchildren visited.

They were all now themselves successful, doing well. Three were married. The nun took her final vows and they all went to the church in Kingston for the occasion. Maas Henry insisted that they all go to a restaurant to celebrate. At the dinner, he made a speech saying that God had given them so much he was happy to give back one of his treasures to God. That quite surprised everyone as that was the first time they had heard him say anything like that. Life was good. It was truly a blessed and happy family.

Then one year, Maas Henry became strangely quiet and looked rather sad. Maas Aleck, his close friend and confidante, was deeply disturbed, till Maas Henry confided to his friend that he would like to visit China before he died to pay respects at his parents' grave. They had died some years before. Maas Aleck was very encouraging, and after some discussion with Alton and Miss Caro it was decided he would go to China. He wanted Miss Caro and Alton and Pearlie and all the grandchildren, in fact the whole family, to go with him. Of course that was not practical, and he had to settle for Jade and his two doctor grandsons to make the trip. And so, at the appointed time, the four of them set off for China.

All went well. The old man took the long plane and ship rides like a trouper. He arrived in China full of enthusiasm. He visited his native village, paid respects to his dead parents and relatives, visited his old school and the old village temple. Modern development had not yet reached them. He saw relatives he had not seen since he left China as a young man. He was visibly ecstatic as he performed the required rituals. At age eighty plus he had come home.

His grandson, named after him, advised him to slow down as he moved from one thing to another and to take it easy. He wouldn't hear of it and seemed so happy and healthy. Jade too, was a little concerned as at one point, she said she thought he looked a bit tired. He organized a big banquet for all his relatives, and many came from nearby villages for the occasion. He drank to their health and long life and prosperity and they in turn wished him the same. There was much feasting and reminiscing with his friends of schooldays, recounting some of the amusing and daring antics they got up to when they were boys. After twelve midnight, he went to bed on the third floor of the old house, a happy and contented man.

At dawn the next morning as the moon dipped behind the lichee trees by the stream at the back of the house, smiling gently, he quietly and peacefully died. His heart had given out as his grandsons had feared. In his little leather pouch that he had purchased for the journey, they found a letter written in the calligraphy of his neat Chinese hand, and when a relative translated it, there were directions on a number of things: where his will was located in Jamaica, what was to be done with his personal things, his watch, his books. He also charged the children and grandchildren to look after their grandmother and be kind to poor people. His expressed wish was to be buried in the little churchyard in Content in Jamaica, the place where he knew that his beloved Caro would want to be, so that they would be together, even as they had been all their adult life. It was however, a mammoth task to get his body back to Jamaica; nevertheless, they decided once more that Goong Goong's wish must be honoured.

And so, on a bleak Sunday afternoon a few weeks later, he was laid to rest in the little churchyard. Present were all his grandchildren, his relatives from Kingston and Montego Bay, and an army of friends and well-wishers from miles around. The village had never seen such a large gathering for a funeral, not ever. Miss Caro was a tower of strength, a regal figure, comforting her sorrowing grandchildren and greeting her sympathizers. She sat on the chair her son had provided for her at the graveside and a single tear rolled down her sorrowing face as Maas Henry was lowered into the grave. She knew that it would not be long before she would be laid beside her beloved companion of over fifty years. True to tradition, and as he would have wished, a large meal was prepared by his friends and served to all who came to the church after the burial.

Want All, Lose All

The calm, quiet village of Palmer's Run woke up this particular morning in June to the news of the war that had broken out between Bucky and Maas James. Bucky was Maas James' nephew. His brother, Maas John was Bucky's father. Few months before, Maas John died and the war was over the family land. What villagers knew as a simmering situation was now boiling over, as the parties concerned made no further secret of the affair.

"It not jus simple so," as Miss Conse pointed out. True, for to understand this quarrel you have to know that family's history. Maas John and Maas James were brothers, but by different mothers. Their father, Papa Tom, was a tom by name and nature. He had other women with whom he had children aside from his wife Miss Millie. Maas John was the only outside son. All the others were girls. John and James were his only two male offspring. But all through their life, it was clear that Maas John was the favourite. People couldn't understand how this could be so. Papa Tom showered this son with all the things that boys liked to have and then some more. Not that he neglected Maas James, or any of his other children for that matter. He was a man known for his full support of all the many children he fathered. Miss Millie had got so used to this that whenever he owned the outside children, she would even see to it that they were properly supported. He had the means, so this was not a problem and many times it was she who passed money and other benefits to the various mothers to whom she was cordial, if not friendly. "She is a saint mi a tell you, Miss Vie," said Miss Conse.

Some said Papa Tom loved Maas John more because he was lighter in complexion than Maas James, or because he was brighter in school, or because he played cricket well and got picked for the school team. Miss Conse, however, said that was not it and none of those reasons was the real one. She knew the real reason. "I would put my neck pon di block Miss Vie, is because of the mother. Im love har caan done. Yu memba how she did pretty?"

Miss Vie had to admit that Maas John's mother, Pearly Johnson, was by far the prettiest young woman ever, in the district. "She was the love of im life and when she had dat pretty little brown boy baby, mi modder say, im walk and strut like a peacock, and when she die some months after wid baby cold, it look like im was going mad. So im try meck up fi dat and spoil Maas John."

The spoiling went as far as to when they were grown up. Papa Tom made it known that the land and property was for the two sons, even though one was a bastard. All these years Mass James made no fuss about it. He had come to an agreement with his brother and seemed content with the arrangement where his mother, the lawful wife, got the house and he and his brother would work the land at opposite sides of the property, separated by the piece with his mother's house, out of each other's way. While Maas John was alive, there was no trouble, but the moment he passed away Maas James began to claim all the land. All the advice he got, to leave well alone, he ignored. He was told that rightly the land belonged to Miss Millie and that he should be content to have the facility of using the piece he was on. Teacher Parkin even advised him to try to buy a little piece for himself as there was John's son Bucky to consider, and everyone knew Bucky was not an easy customer. He even advised Miss Millie to seek legal advice and settle the matter, as if in prophesy "to avoid blood shed".

Maas James paid no attention to all this advice. His mother also advised him to come to some agreement with his nephew. She was all for settling the matter peacefully "for blood thicker dan water", but he wanted all the land for himself and agreement was out of the question. He sent a message to Bucky at Christmas to inform him that he was giving him six months to get off the land. During the six months he should clear off all his cultivation, as after that if he was caught on the land he wouldn't be responsible for what happened. Naturally, Bucky was outraged and sent back a message to his uncle telling him that if he wanted a war he was ready. It would seem that all the secret resentment Maas James harboured against his half brother was now being transferred to his nephew.

So the enmity and the hatred went back and forth with no resolution, not even dialogue between them, for they stopped speaking to each other and were at daggers drawn.

What happened on that day was no surprise. A cow belonging to Bucky, strayed over to Maas James' side of the land. He promptly caught the animal and chopped it, in an attempt to kill it. The attempt proved successful, for by the time Bucky discovered that the cow had gone astray, he got the news that it had gone over to Maas James and that he had nearly chopped off its head. Bucky did not even stop to put on his trousers. He had been lounging around that afternoon in his underpants and had no shirt on. In his bare underpants, he stormed over to Maas James who was standing near the now dead cow, cutlass in hand, still wet with the blood of the animal.

What transpired was to go down in the history of the village as the start of the worst time they had ever seen. As Bucky advanced to his uncle, he let out a barrage of bad words describing the act and the person who committed it in the foulest language imaginable, with Maas James shouting back in like manner, matching Bucky word for foul word. Soon the yard was full of spectators and the shouting match now took on an uglier tone as the cursing now moved from the two men to their respective families. Maas James described Bucky as a bastard, the son of a whore and a bastard. That made Bucky so angry that he shouted back, "A whofa madda yu a call whore, a yu Coolie wife a whore, yu dutty johncrow yu." With that, Maas James advanced on him, cutlass raised, and people gasped and screamed, "No Mass James, no!" Bucky wrenched a yam stick from the newly planted yam hill nearest to him, and with it quickly moved to the machete wielder who chopped furiously at the yam stick which Bucky deftly wielded, disarming him, and the machete fell some distance away. It was quickly picked up and hidden by one of the men in the crowd.

Seeing this, Bucky threw down the yam stick and now the two men faced each other with bare hands, still shouting threats and obscenities at each other. Soon they were wrestling and hitting each other till blood was coming from Maas James' nose. The people around shouted at them to stop, to no avail, and the fight continued for several minutes. The older man soon tired, clearly no match for his nephew who had the advantage of youth and strength. The outcome of the fight was certain and Miss Conse begged the men watching to part them before Bucky got himself in serious trouble. "Im goin kill im." Seeing that no one would help, she grabbed hold of a boy and said to him, "Run go call Corpral," and the youngster took off in the direction of the police station.

By now, Bucky's thin cotton underpants was down to his ankles and he kicked it off, making him stark naked to the amusement of some of the onlookers. But the fight went on. Bucky now had Maas James down in the mud, raining blow after blow all over his body and try as he might he couldn't free himself as the younger man had him pinned to the ground. It really seemed as though the outcome would be serious as Maas James, after a while, showed little sign of resistance or retaliation.

Just when everyone was sure he would be seriously hurt, Corporal arrived with a blue seam officer and took charge. "Unno stop the damn fighting or ah goin to arrest the two of you, stop it, bruck it up." He motioned to the other officer and the two of them managed to pull the naked Bucky off Maas James. Two men helped him to his feet and, as he tried to move toward Bucky, Corporal shouted, "Hole im!" The men complied.

Corporal having parted them gave them a good talking to and cautioned that if they did not desist, he would lock them both up and charge them with a number of offences. He ended by saying, "The two of you are blood relatives, that must mean something." He ordered Bucky to put back on his underpants. "Put on yu clothes and go home and don't meck a see yu back here again. Since the cow was trespassing, all yu can do is meck use of the meat. Call butcher Francis, and I order you Maas James to allow them to deal with it so he can at least recover some of the cost of the animal. And for God's sake, stop the fighting and the warring." With that, Corporal left and since Maas James said nothing, everyone thought that was the end of that.

Bucky recovered nearly the whole value of the animal from the sale of the carcass, including the skin, so he pretty soon cooled down. Miss Millie insisted that Maas James and Bucky accompany her to the lawyer, and it seemed things would be settled peacefully. They agreed on what she thought was a fair division of the property and begged them to forget the past. All went well for a few weeks but all this time Maas James was seething with hatred. Even though he had agreed to the division he was secretly very angry. How could his mother agree to give away part of his father's land to his bastard son's family? All the pleading of his mother and others for peace was in vain. The more they pleaded, the more angry he became, though he kept this to himself. Revenge was now his obsession, but not even his wife suspected that. Not only had Bucky called his wife a whore, he had given him a sound beating in front of the whole village.

All seemed to be going well until…the first of August picnic was in full swing at the community centre, and everyone was having a great time. Music from the village band accompanied the children at the Maypole where the adults on the side were urging and instructing the young dancers while doing a merry jig in tune with the music. Elsewhere on the grounds, groups of children played ring games, a group of boys played bat and ball. At the makeshift bar, the men gathered as usual, drinking their favourites.

Bucky and a few of his friends were having a merry time when Maas James approached. He was greeted quite friendly by everyone and offered a drink. He accepted the bottle of stout, drank it quietly, saying nothing, calmly putting the empty bottle on the counter near where Bucky was. All this while he was eyeing Bucky, but no one paid any attention as his eyes followed his nephew. Suddenly, before anyone knew what was happening, he plunged the ten inch kitchen knife he had cleverly concealed into Bucky's chest, piercing his heart.

The young man collapsed on the ground, bleeding, not uttering a sound. In a few minutes he was dead, his eyes wide open and with the knife still in his body. What followed was much confusion, shouting and yelling. Some of the men tried to hold Maas James, fearing he might try to escape. That was unnecessary, as he slowly walked to the big stone under the breadnut tree and calmly sat down staring into space. That is where the Corporal found him. "What foolishness is this Maas James...What foolishness? Come!"

Miss Conse, through her tears said, "Im boun fi heng... poor Miss Millie...Im won't even get six foot six of di lan, for dem bury dem a Spanish Town. Want all lose all."

Taming the Beast

"It serve her right mi dear Miss Vie. Much as mi sympathise wid her, she had no business leaving the comfort of her granny house an gone to live wid that brute beast in a dat little ole wappen-bappen room beside an ole bruckdung kitchen." Miss Conse was livid, for she had just seen Clarice at Dr. Powell's surgery with clear evidence of another beating from Gladstone. This time, however, it seemed worse than all the other times. "What is even more hurtful, the pickney gal come offa good table, she let dung her fambly bad bad."

"All di same, im have no right to treat har so, but she name woman, an some man is a biease," Miss Vie ventured.

"A brute bease ah tell yu. Yu si mi, dats why I live my life widdout depending on any a dem, mi live my life widdout dem." Miss Conse, a confirmed spinster, was known for her independence and proud life and was often heard to speak her mind how she felt about some of the men she knew. "A not talking about man like Maas Butty, but you have some man whey wicked and terrible in more ways dan one."

Miss Vie was quick to defend her husband of over twenty-five years. "No mam, from I know Butty for over thirty years an wi married for twenty-seven, im never raise im voice to mi much more im han."

"Because im is a good man, an know how fi treat woman Yu know the story of how im father use to treat him mother Aunty Fan, people used to sey, like a queen. Dat ole bwoy Gladstone is a heartless cruff."

Clarice had told her that, yesterday, Gladstone had come home from work two hours earlier than the usual, at four instead of six, and raised eternal hell because the food was not ready. He cursed her in the worst way, telling her how lazy she was, that he worked very hard, was supporting her, and that the least she could do was to see that he got his food when he came home.

"But yu come home extra early today, di six a clock Corchie no even blow yet." When she heard the sound each day she would know that she had a good fifteen minutes before he would arrive. "Mi neva expec yu so soon, you neva tell mi sey you coming home this early. Anyway, the food soon ready."

"Yu shudda did know," he bellowed, "an no gi mi none a yu fasty back chat." With that, he slapped her cross her mouth and proceeded to give her the beating of her life, which as it turned out, seemed to have left her with a broken rib and, according to Dr. Powell, battered muscles, a black eye, bruised face, and maybe, hopefully, not some internal injuries to her kidneys and intestines.

Poor Clarice, young, foolish at the age of nineteen she left her grandmother's comfortable home where she had her own spacious room, nice and well furnished, to live with Gladstone, her new-found lover. He had come from the neighbouring parish to work at the factory, this handsome and dashing young man of the world. It was not long that he met Clarice and soon the two of them "got een". This young innocent girl was completely taken with him. He was her first. They would meet secretly and, for a while, no one really knew. When her grandmother found out, she was angry, as among other things, she was told Gladstone was known in his home place as a woman beater. That was the reason the last girlfriend left him, even though it was said he had offered her marriage. The time they were spending living together was a sort of test to ascertain if she would do as a wife. It was also said that that was his way – offer the girlfriends marriage, and hold that over them. But really, he had no intention of ever marrying anyone.

When he moved to the district, he rented the little room from Uncle Levi, who had fixed up his buttery adjoining the kitchen. The little room was cramped and could not even accommodate a conventional bed. But he made a frame attached to the wall in the corner and put a makeshift mattress on it and that is where the silly girl chose to leave her home and come to live with her cunning lover. It became the talk of the village.

For two months all was calm and sweet. Some persons, even though they did not approve, hoped and prayed that he would treat her right. Her grandmother especially, prayed daily for her, and even called a prayer meeting in her house to "put her case before the Cross", and she never stopped praying for her granddaughter. But three months had not

passed since she came to live with him, when he started to beat her regularly, and for the slightest thing, even when the fault was clearly his. She seemed to like what was going on, for when Miss Conse asked her why she put up with it she said, "Is because im love mi why." But according to Mr. Larkie, the old police corporal, "Some man beat woman fi pleasure. When me was in di force, the brain doctor tell mi sey it sweet some man when dem beat woman, it pleasure dem."

But the common talk among many women was that it was love why they were being battered. As twisted as that thinking was, day after day, week after week, month after month, Clarice became a part of the women being regularly beaten by their men. Until well into the second year of their affair, the beating continued and intensified until she, like many other women, expected it and took it for nothing, in fact some wore the scars proudly like trophies. "Nutten no go so, a fool dem fool and wortlis," said Miss Conse to some women in the market.

Dr. Powell was sure that, on this occasion, he had gone too far and asked her to come back the following day, when he would do a more thorough examination. She was to try to get Gladstone to bring her; he didn't have to work on Sundays. In the meantime, she was to take the painkillers he prescribed and stay in bed as much as possible. She left the doctor's office, wondering how she was going to get Gladstone to take her to the doctor, and that night she prayed that she would find a way. When her granny heard of the incident, she was down on her knees again, begging her God to help her.

Next morning Clarice stayed on the makeshift bed they shared, and started to groan heavily, complaining for pain in her chest and her right thigh. She did so well at the groaning that he seemed to be sympathetic.

"Den is what do yu now?" he asked her. "The tablets no meck yu feel better?"

"No Gladdy you haffi carry mi back to Doctor today, ah can't meck it on mi own."

"Mi no know how dat a go go yu know for mi did wan go a river wid dem odder man…an look pon mi han, it look like it sprain, seeit a swell."

She raised up, took his hand and said, "Lawd a true yu know." That was the reason she needed, the answer to her prayer. "Gladdy yu have to go to Doctor," she said as she caressed his sprained hand. It didn't take much to persuade this vain young man to go to the doctor with his mildly injured hand.

At the doctor's office in the afternoon, Gladstone had to endure the cut eyes and the silence from most of the other people waiting. No doubt they had heard of this latest beating, but that was nothing compared to the tongue lashing that he got from the old Doc. After carefully attending to them and giving them advice to assist in the healing process, Doc said to Gladstone, "Do you see what your bad temper and cruelty has caused? I don't want you to ever try that again, because I won't be attending to either of you if you cause each other any more bodily harm. You are lucky there are no serious internal injuries. The rib is not really broken, just bruised and it will soon heal. Next time, you will hire a car and go to the hospital. You know young man, this could be a police case if I report it. But I am advising you, no I am warning you, be careful, because if this happens again, I myself will go to the police."

Gladstone made no reply. Clarice thanked the doctor and when the nurse told them how much they had to pay, Gladstone was shocked. It was a guinea each. He paid the fees as he had brought enough money, but on the way home he cursed Clarice, "Yu si how much yu cost mi?"

She said nothing but secretly thought, "Is your fault."

Clarice, true to her resolve, did all she could to please him in and out of bed. She catered to his every whim and fancy and then some more and for a while things seemed to be running smoothly and peacefully, and even though he would make a fuss and quarrel sometimes, he kept his hands off her.

"I remember what Doc say, but don't form the ass, or else!" he frequently warned her.

When Miss Conse heard, she was happy. "Miss Vie, it look like Gladstone stop beat Clarice, is a good while now a don't hear that im put im han pon her. I would advise him not to. I hear Dr. Powell warn im good."

"Ahi Miss Conse," Miss Vie sighed, "I really hope so, but speckle fowl can't turn leghorn, time longer dan rope."

Miss Conse laughed, "Yu never dun eeh Miss Vie, but we will si." And Granny Sue kept praying.

All was well till "Firse a Agas" grand market. Clarice was in the market buying her supplies. She went to the scallion lady from St. Elizabeth and there was Miss Conse.

"Clarice, how things?"

"Not bad Miss Conse."

She made her purchase in silence, said her goodbyes to Miss Conse and was on her way.

"Poor girl," Miss Conse said and proceeded to tell the lady the story of how she was being ill treated by this man. She gave her the whole bill and receipt, the whole doona pan full. The lady sighed and, apart from a few questions, listened attentively and in silence. Miss Conse ended with, "some woman have fi live through hell doh eeh." To this the lady sighed again.

On her way out of the market, Clarice was passing the lady, who called her, "Come here young lady, I want to tell yu something." Clarice went over to her. "I live through the same thing you a feel now when I was a young woman." She recounted how, as a young woman, her husband was in the habit of battering her for the simplest thing. Until one day ,after years of sufferation, she found a way to make him stop. It was her grandmother, a maroon lady, who gave her the advice which she proceeded to give Clarice.

She pulled Clarice down to her until the girl's ear was close to her mouth, as she sat on the little board stool in front of her load of produce, and whispered in her ear. No one heard what she said. She placed a salad tomato in her basket and said, "Memba what a tell yu, si yu nex week," and Clarice walked away with a spring in her step and a smile on her lips.

All the way home she plotted, smiling to herself. The first thing she decided to do was to cook beef soup for dinner instead of beef stew as she usually did on Saturdays, for she well knew that Gladstone hated soup, especially beef soup with pumpkin. He said it reminded him of what he saw in baby's diapers. The whole neighbourhood could hear Clarice singing as she cooked the specially disliked soup. She went about it as if it were his favourite meal. Why she was singing, no one knew, but she sang loudly and clearly a number of songs, including "We shall overcome".

As was expected, Gladstone came home quite hungry that Saturday afternoon and when the soup was placed before him on the table in the corner of the little room, he flew into a rage, quickly getting out of control. "Clarice!" he bellowed. "What the hell is dis woman, what yu give mi fi mi dinna dis big Satiday?"

She replied with mocked innocence, "Is nice beef soup wid pumpkin. You don't like it?"

"Yu know blasted well that ah don't drink no other soup except peas soup. Ah don't drink no damn punkin soup whe fava baby shit, wha happen to di stew beef?"

"Well mi cook beef soup, if yu don't like it, tough. Go a road go fine something else, bulla dey a shop," Clarice said and ended with a laugh.

Who told her to say that? Gladstone jumped up, bellowing, "Yu bitch yu, yu do it just to provoke mi," and he advanced to Clarice who faced him defiantly.

"So what yu going to do about it?" She was now standing in the kitchen doorway.

"Is anadder backsidein yu want tidday?"

Clarice taunted him, "If yu tink yu bad touch mi". She taunted him as she brandished the kitchen knife.

"Teck that!" and he shot her a box, grabbed her around her neck, and pitched her against the wall, disarming her. The knife she was holding fell to the concrete floor.

Clarice bawled out, "Whai, whai, murder, police, murder, help."
This was the very first time that she cried out while he was beating her. Gladstone kept beating her and she kept calling out, "Gladdy a kill mi…whoi…help…murder, police!"

The more she cried, the more he battered her, he did not let up. With one movement, he pulled her off the kitchen wall and threw her down on the ground almost knocking her breath out of her.

"Yu want a kill you rahtid tidday?" He was now straddling her, towering over her as she lay on the ground. He raised his right foot ready to kick her in her side.

Clarice remembered the advice the lady in the market gave her, or maybe she was thinking of it all along as she clearly begged for this bout of beating and was waiting on the right moment. So she reached up and firmly grabbed both his testicles in a dead hold and commenced to wring them in her tight grasp from which he could not escape.

This immediately and completely immobilized the six foot tall brute of a giant, and he became a little puppy dog in her hand. "Whey yu a du...let mi go...let mi go a sey!" She held on, tightening her grip all the while twisting her hand. "Clarice...leggo mi seed.". She twisted tighter.

"Lawd Gad, a dead now, whai...whai...Clarice you likkle bitch yu, a kill yu waan kill mi...Let mi go a sey... whai, whai!" So he bawled, so she tightened her death grip until his voice broke, "Lawd...help...somebody help...do Clarry do... let mi go nuh...a likkle joke mi did a meck... whai...whai," his strong booming voice reduced to almost a whimper. All this time she didn't say a word.

In vain he begged and pleaded. By now people began to gather to witness what was happening. First the ones in the yard, then from both sides next door, from across the road, over the tailor shop and the shoemaker shop, people passing to and from market, even the children from over the Chinese shop. Gladstone was in agony, "Lawd Clarry, lawd!"

He spotted Miss Gatta and Brother Manny, the farrier, in the crowd and called out to them, "Lawd Miss Gatta talk to her, meck she let mi go nuh," and as Clarice squeezed a little harder"Wai wai." Miss Gatta scornfully replied, "Mi a midwife, mi a noh police." He appealed to Brother Manny, "Lawd Bredda Manny help mi nuh, meck her let mi go, Lawd do sah." The crowd laughed and jeered at the spectacle, "Look how she have im." "Serve him right, cruel bease! The wicked wretch."

By this, Clarice had managed to get up, still holding on firmly to her prize and she proceeded to lead him all over the yard, as if to ensure that all those gathered saw his humiliation. Crouched in pain and calling out for help, he reluctantly followed her like a little lap dog, calling now in a voice broken to a mere whisper, "Help mi somebody help mi

...Clarry a mi yu a treat so? Lawd unno have mercy pon mi nuh!" Needless to say no one was anxious to help him, for time and time again they had watched him ill treating, abusing and battering the poor girl. When it looked as if he couldn't bear the pain any more, Brother Manny and Pa Jim decided to try to get her to let him go. Try as they might they couldn't break the "dead-hole", though they tried to pry her fingers loose. "Come Miss Clarry, you punish im enough, ease im up, have pity on im," Brother Manny pleaded with her. "Mine you get yuself inna trouble wid the law," advised Pa Jim, "Im mus learn im lesson by now."

Clarice broke her silence and spoke for the first time. "All right mista man, I want to hear yu swear in front of all dese people, dat you will never raise yu han at me or any other woman again, as long as yu live."

"Yes mi dear, a promise."

"I never say promise, ah say swear, swear."

"Ah swear that I will never lick yu as long as a live. Nor any odder woman," Clarice prompted.

"Ah swear dat if a lick yu or any odder woman may mi right han widdered up or rotten off." Gladstone dutifully swore as she dictated and when he had so sworn, Clarice added, "So help mi God."

"All that too Clarry".

She twisted her wrist as hard as she could and he yelled, "Wahai wahai, so help mi God," to which the crowd in unison replied, "Amen!"

With that, the now triumphant Clarice released her captive with a grand gesture that all could see, and the cheering from the crowd could be heard from a good distance around, giving full endorsement of her action. Gladstone, still in pain, sank down to the ground where he had been standing, still groaning from the pain. "Ohi Ohi!"

Miss Conse who had arrived earlier and was watching from the shade of the orange tree, hugged Clarice. "Girl a proud a yu, proud proud. Look whey mi live fi si, yu tame di beas today day, di brute! Woman power teck im tidday. And look how she so likkle bit. Big enough to hold im life ina one han."

Brother Manny was sympathetic to the young man. "As man to man Gladstone, yu should go to the Doctor, for yu don't know the extent of the damage, and you have to be careful, especially to dat part of yu body."

"True sah, true for it still a hurt mi bad."

He took the advice and within an hour was sitting in Dr. Powell's office. By that time, Doctor had heard the news of what happened, as had the whole village, and as Granny Sue heard it she was down on her knees again.

If Gladstone was expecting sympathy from the Doc he was mistaken. Doctor Powell was pleased as anyone else that at last the young woman had acted, all be it in a serious way. But Doctor had seen enough of the abuse he and other men inflicted on their women whom they professed to care for.

The examination on Gladstone revealed that there was no real permanent damage. Other than bruises to the testes, the scrotum and spermatic cords, no serious damage was detected. He was to rest and not harass himself, and it meant no sex till the pain had gone, for only then could he be sure that everything was properly healed.

"How long it will teck to get better Doc?" he asked.

"About three to four weeks."

Gladstone groaned again at the thought of no sex for a month. Doctor Powell also reminded him of the last time before that when he warned him about his behaviour and bad temper.

"If yu know what good for yu stop it."

Later when he spoke to Maas Alton, Gladstone confessed that he thought he was dying, the pain was so severe.

Early that night, there was a knock on Granny Sue's door. "Ah who dat?" the old lady asked from her bedside prayers.

"Ah me Clarry, granny."

"God be praised, the prodigal return, come in chile, come in, come in."

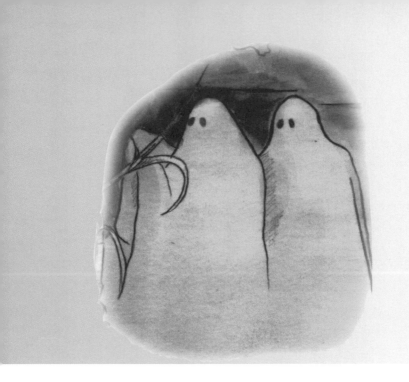

Pyjama Sport

Morning broke calm and sunny on the hill overlooking the quiet village of Davy Pass. The morning mist quickly got out of the way of the beautiful warm sunshine, and soon the whole peaceful valley was bathed in the splendid glow of a June morning.

Miss Pauline, Maas Clinton's wife, was up early while the surroundings were still in the half light before the sun came up. She had to be. Even before the sun peeped over the breadnut tree at the back of her house she had already lit the Etna and made the usual cup of brewed coffee for her young lover Philbert, son of the Pastor from over Bull Run. This tall, well-built, muscular young man was known by the whole area as a skilled and hardworking carpenter, much in

demand. He was also known secretly by many ladies as a lover of gigantic proportion and skill, much in demand. Though each one of his many conquests did not talk of this to anyone, least of all among themselves, they each secretly, thought they were the only one who knew at first hand and by experience of his attributes and prowess. They kept the secret well they thought, and he did too. Quite unlike his friends, he did not speak a word of all his carryings on. He couldn't afford to; he took some serious chances. But as will always happen in matters of the kind, people began to whisper. Soon the whole village knew the "secret". Miss Conse who knew everything remarked, "Is a open secret Miss Vie, open secret."

He moved from woman to willing woman, who he fancied and when he fancied. Strangely, none of them got pregnant, so rumour had it that he was sterile. As Miss Conse told the story, there was a mumps epidemic when he was about twelve and he had a very bad attack of the disease. The doctor managed to save his testicles, but said that it had been so bad he was sure he was never going to be able to father children. "Me remember that time and plenty children got the mumps doh me never get it," Miss Conse concluded.

That, it seemed, gave the young man the license to do as he liked, when and how he liked with as many women as he liked and not have to worry about the consequences. Well, he had been doing this for many years with young and not so young women, fat and slim, married and single, anyone who would allow him, and there were many ready and willing, those who dreamed of him. Few, though, could satisfy him to the point where he would return to their beds. That is, until the day he met this certain lady.

Miss Pauline had moved to the village about two years ago with her husband who was much older than herself. As soon as she saw Philbert she liked him right away and spent many nights in her lonely bed fantasizing, with the young stallion as the object of her fantasy. She had a trim, attractive body which Philbert found extremely enticing and which he rather admired and liked, but she bided her time, planning, knowing one day one day...so it was not long before they became lovers. Strangely, he was faithful to her, seeing no one else but her at the time, to the annoyance of his other ladies, because he liked what happened when they were together and he kept coming back for more. They were two of a kind it seemed, seeking excitement and physical satisfaction. Matter of fact, it was rumoured that her husband was now almost useless in that department. The fact that his job took him away from home days at a time, sometimes for a whole week, only made matters worse and served to facilitate her activities with her lover.

But she was very clever, so her doting husband thought all was "sweetness and light". He didn't dream of what was happening. He didn't have a clue about what the whole village knew: that as soon as his work truck picked him up to go on one of his many jobs, sometimes thirty miles away, Philbert only waited as long for the cover of night to find himself up the hill to the neat little house, quite secluded, occupied by this husband and wife of over ten years. Miss Pauline married her husband when she was just about twenty-one, and he was near fifty.

Things worked well for a time, but the years and the diabetes medication were not kind to him and, according to Miss Conse, "It seems like these last few years she have to get help when nature call."

Philbert fitted the bill perfectly. This whole affair all started when he got the job to do some repairs on their house and Maas Clinton suggested that, since he would be there in the days to act as the "Hole Yah", he could spare himself the expense of bringing the apprentice. He didn't think that there would be days when he would not be there and Philbert would be alone with Miss Pauline – just the opportunity they wanted. From the very first encounter, they both knew that they had found what that they were looking for, that would not be the last and that this would go on for a long time, and so it did.

The only person who did not seem to know what was going on was Maas Clinton. Miss Conse confided to Miss Julia, "But im mus know. Ah wonder if im know and jus a play fool fi ketch wise, or maybe im appreciate the help."

Miss Julia laughed, "That might well be so ascordin to what I hear."

Miss Pauline was quite contented with her young man, but as a ploy she kept up the complaining about the amount of time Maas Clinton was away from home and things went on without any disruption for a while, but as Miss Conse remarked, "Wha done inna darkness boun to come out inna light."

Maas Clinton, this day, left as usual to go to a job at Buck Up. He was a water engineer expert on water pumps. When he boarded the truck, Miss Pauline, with pretended sadness asked him, "How long this time honey?"

"Three, four days, maybe a week, the ole pump bruck dung, I will send you a message."

Then he was off. Pauline thought with a smile, "Three day, one week, all the same."

As usual, Philbert was right on spot as it got dark. He came up the hill by the back as usual and they didn't waste any time. She gave him his customary drink of two bottles of Cock stout mixed with condensed milk and plenty nutmeg. Soon the lamps were put out, except the one turned down low in the bedroom, so it was quite dark. Then they settled down to merriment and the stillness was interrupted only by their sighing and moaning and heavy breathing and the crickets and toads outside.

Just before day-morning, just before second cock crow, Philbert was on his way to work, only to return at night fall, night after night, to repeat the happenings. According to Miss Conse, "So damn boldface."

Well, Miss Pauline got no message from Maas Clinton, so this time around, after the second night, she felt everything was fine and she didn't think he would be home before the end of the week. So, on the third night it was business as usual. And this night, after a hard bout of lovemaking, they both fell asleep, out like a light.

The particular job Mass Clinton was on, however, finished days quicker than he had said it would. Instead of having the tedious task of repairing the pump, he just had to install the new one, as his boss had decided that the old one was not worth repairing since it was quite old and troublesome. This took much less time than the repairs and, that night, at around eleven o'clock he arrived home. Wanting to surprise his wife, he tiptoed on the verandah to the side door which was always left unlocked, opened it quietly and entered the sitting hall as quiet as a mouse. As he paused and waited he could hear the snoring coming from the bedroom. "She always snore when she sleep sound," he thought, so he was extra quiet as he peeped into the bedroom through the slightly open door, but was not prepared for what he saw. He saw his wife snugly in the arms of another man, both sleeping the kind of sleep that only came after pleasure.

In the dim light of the room, he saw them plainly, though he could not make out who the man was, but he could make out that he had on his favourite pyjamas. He watched for a while, then quietly he lit the lamp in the sitting hall and flung the door open so the light from that lamp flooded the bedroom. He shouted, "Pauline a which man dat you have inna mi bed?"

They both jumped up, and Philbert was out of the bed in a flash. He grabbed his clothes from the chair beside the bed and was out of the room, onto the verandah and out into the bushes, fast like greased lightning, still wearing Maas Clinton's pyjamas, leaving Miss Pauline alone to face her angry husband. He saw the man but could not really tell for certain who it was, though he had his suspicion. Maas Clinton was beside himself with rage, "Soh a dat a gwan when I out there bussing mi ass to give you a comfortable home. How yu could do dat to me? How yu could do dat to yuself?"

She had no answer for her distraught partner but she said later to her best friend, "What im expect mi to do? Is almost two year now im can't function properly. Nutten naw gwan, for when im do try is greef an torture mi a tell yu."

Her friend, as could be expected, was sympathetic, "Ahi mi dear, every heart know its own sorrow."

Then with an impish smile she asked, "Den is who was in yu bed?"

And as friend to friend, she let the puss out of the bag, "Who but Philbert! "

"Philbert!!! That's why ah don't see that brute fa more dan two year now. Im is the bess. Ah can't blame yu."

But Miss Conse was not that kind, "She wukless fi carry man in her husband married bed, dem kina woman is just pretty face an rotten cloth."

When the story spread, it was not long before Miss Pauline left the village and they heard that she had first gone to Kingston to her mother, and later she left to America to her sister. It was not long before Philbert was applying for his passport. Miss Conse wished them well and as for Maas Clinton, "All the same, it serve him right, a so nuff a dem ole man married young gal an expect dat dem can take care of business for any length of time."

He, in his embarrassment, sold the house and went to live in Westmoreland where he had a grown-up son. He did not speak a word of the incident till his schoolmate, who he had not seen for thirty or more years, arrived from Colon and enquired for his wife. He told the story of the divorce, and in the telling Maas Clinton bared his soul, "Imagine me come home sudden in a middle night and find a man inna mi bedroom, inna mi bed, wid mi wife, an if dat was not enough, di man inna mi pyjama."

Not So Lord, Not So

Come to think of it, they were regarded by the village as well-off, even as aristocrats by some of the poorer villagers, and most people in and around the surrounding areas regarded them as upper class, and even high class.

To begin with, they were of light brown complexion and had "good hair". They were the descendants of a group of privileged persons who were known as "money people" who owned much land from way back, which this brother and sister in their early seventies had inherited. They were all that was left of this once proud and wealthy family. The older people in the area remembered the family of yesteryears as people who "had it", people of substance.

They were cattle-breeders, and on their vast acreage they had many tenant farmers whose annual rental amounted to a substantial income. All in all, it was a well-to-do family, now represented by the surviving brother and sister.

They both played the piano and they loved music, and as they fancied, took turns playing their favourites for hours at a time. He was the better musician, well, more flamboyant, playing with much flourish. She, however, was more steady, constant. A regular churchgoer, she sometimes played the old pipe organ in the Anglican Church. That was a real treat, not so much for the music, but for the gyrations and manoeuvers she had to make to reach the pedals, to the amusement of all who saw her. Up to a few years ago she taught a number of students who could afford to pay. On occasions she would fix flowers for the altar in her church and she was the registrar of births and deaths.

He, on the other hand, was a ne'er-do-well alcoholic who did nothing but eat, drink white rum and sleep, and he depended on his sister for everything, clothing, his daily sustenance of food, shelter and the occasional money to feed his drinking habit. He seemed never to work a day in his life, and at this stage was considered hopeless and useless. She controlled the family purse and what resources and property they had, and everyone knew she was as tight as that unmentionable part of the duck's anatomy.

Their otherwise quiet and calm genteel life was occasionally interrupted by outbursts of temper tantrums, especially when he wanted his drink and she refused. This was chiefly on Friday afternoons when he knew that she had collected money. And if the end of the month was a Friday, you could bet he would loudly make his demands in no uncertain manner. On such occasions, people passing on the nearby road would stop to listen to the fuss, and they were sure that one day something serious would happen.

She would say nothing, but would sit at the old, out of tune piano and play for as long as he was ranting and raving, and just when it seemed that something physical would happen, came the big crescendo from both piano and his voice and he managed to calm down. Then she would give him his desire. All to the good, because her frail constitution could hardly stand up to a good puff of breeze.

As she moved about the village, people regarded her with mixed feelings, "Look pon di mean ole bitch, why she won't just let go the money and give her poor brodder and buy some clothes geem, look how him shabby."

"Im clean doh, di helper wash him clothes dem."

"Mus be once a month, you ever smell im how im smell a stale piss."

"She too wicked an mean." Others were sympathetic towards her. Like Miss Conse, who remembered that they were both in the same class at primary school, "Poor Miss Claudine, look how she put up wid im all dese years, wuckliss. If a me mi run him."

Once, when he stole quite a bit of money from her, some said she should lock him up. Others said she had more than she needed so she shouldn't complain. She did report it to Corporal at the Police Station, because he had threatened to harm her, but when the police came for him she said she changed her mind and wouldn't press charges as he had not really hit or done her any bodily harm. Again, Miss Conse had her say, "She miss her chance to get rid of him."

Things went pretty smoothly after that; what with the stolen money he had more than enough white rum to drink. She begged him not to drink so much, but to her pleadings he paid no attention and spent most of the days in a drunken stupour. He barely ate, asking for soup at practically every dinnertime. She became worried and even spoke to the doctor who advised her there was nothing he could do. His few friends too were worried, and Mr. Nash, the tailor, most concerned, pleaded with him, "Mack you caa'n go awn so, yu haffi eat and lay off a di heavy rum drinkin, it not good fah yu, yu killin yu self."

All that pleading and those of others fell on deaf ears. He said nothing to his friends, but every time his sister opened her mouth and tried to talk sense to him – "Mack please cut down on the drinking, even for a while, eat your food and get back your strength" – his only response was to curse her most disgracefully, "Oh shut yu blasted mouth, yu ole hige, leave me alone and go and attend to your damn cows. You regard them more than me anyway."

He knew she had a soft spot for her cattle, especially the milking cows which were her pride and joy. She, along with her two handymen, managed to keep them in such good shape they were admired by all and were the envy of all the other farmers around.

"Go away from me, before a kick yu mawga backside down the stairs and break yu damn neck," he bellowed at her, and maybe he would have done just that, but the helper and one of the handymen were always there when he started to curse her to make sure he did nothing of the kind.

"Lord have mercy," she wailed. "What have I done to deserve this…this cross. Lord, please help me and let this bitter cup pass from me." As usual she ended up at the piano. This seemed to comfort her and silence him, and pretty soon he was snoring loudly and sleeping soundly.

This went on for years, till one day the "cup did pass". It was the day the village and the country received the great news that Germany had surrendered, ending World War II. Everyone celebrated the good news in their own way. Miss Katie broke and roasted a bushel basket full of corn from her field and gave all and sundry who passed by. Maas Joslyn brought out the biggest bunch of ripe bananas you have ever seen and took it to the school gate, for the children who were marching with the Union Jack and singing British patriotic songs. Benjie, the soup man, cooked two kerosene pans full of his famous Cow Darling soup and gave free cups of his special brew to all who wanted it.

Many, including Mack, found the bar and proceeded to try to drink as if they could drink out the stock dry. They drank till they were all properly drunk. They sang war songs at the top of their lungs, "It's a long way to Tipperary, it's a long way to go". When they had exhausted that, they sang "Rule Britannia" and then "From the halls of Montezuma to the shores of Tripoli", and they ended with the singing of "God save the king". Finally, in the late evening, they staggered out of the bar and headed home, not knowing their mother from a broomstick. Miss Claudine heard that her brother was coming up the road, staggering from side to side. Fearing that he would be hit down by a passing vehicle, she sent her handyman Percy to fetch him.

Leaning very heavily on Percy, he reached home but he was unable to make it upstairs to his room. Percy helped him to the narrow daybed in the little room off the sitting hall, pulled his belt and his pants waist and left him making some strange snoring sounds as he fell fast asleep.

Miss Claudine had her supper alone and was off to her bed, kneeling by her bedside as usual for her prayers. This night she begged God to take charge of her brother and release him from the bondage of the rum bar. "Dear Lord, stop him from drinking," she prayed.

She slept soundly, somewhat comforted by her prayers and was awake at the crack of dawn. She dressed and went downstairs to meet Clarice, the helper, and get her morning coffee. She reached the foot of the stairs just in time to hear

Clarice cry out, "Jesus Saviour pilot me!" Miss Claudine hurried to her, leaning on the old sofa in the corner opposite the daybed. There on the floor, was her brother flat on his back, dead, his eyes still wide open, showing just the white portion of his eyeball. She bent down and closed his eyes as Clarice yelled, "Im dead Miss Claudine, im dead dead!"

The autopsy showed that he died from a massive heart attack. His heart had given out with all that drinking he had done the evening before. "Di white rum cut im heart string," was the opinion of Maas Claudy, his friend. Miss Claudine wailed, "Lord have mercy!" She reached down and, to everyone's amazement and surprise, kissed him on his forehead. "Just last night I begged God to take him in charge, just last night I ask God to release him, but not so Lord, not so!" She continued her wailing till Clarice helped her to a chair on the verandah. "Not so Lord, not so!" She was still wailing up to eight o'clock when Miss Conse arrived and comforted her with the words, "I know yu feel it Miss Claudine, for blood thicker dan water. At lease im won't give you any more trouble. Gawd move in a mysterious way and sometime in a mischeevious way."

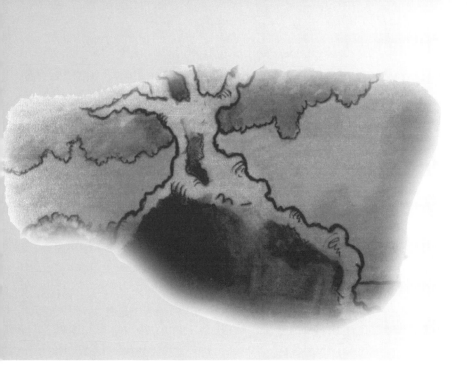

Gungo Soup Remedy

Maas Isaac and Miss Clarry were married in their forties and lived together happily for over twenty-six years. They had an only son who was their pride and joy, but Jacob was born with some kind of defect, brain-wise, so the doctor said, which prevented him from developing normally. The whole district knew that he was not a normal person. Sometimes he behaved like a seven year old, this young man who was well over twenty.

Some persons, unkind and unsympathetic, said that he was a "half idiot" and the teasing and taunting began from he was a little boy at school. Others, less cruel, though he was not treated like a normal child, were kind to him and there were even those who would protect him and look after

him. A few of his boyhood friends would even go to the extreme of fighting off those who would taunt and provoke him. He grew up to be a quiet, shy youngster, "bashful", as Miss Conse often said of him.

"You can't blame him yu know, is because his mother had im so late – old people musn't have children yu know Miss Vie, it not good, for the children born with all kina defect."

Living with a devoted mother and father, he lacked nothing, and his parents lavished their love on him as if to compensate for his condition. He, in turn, was obedient and dutiful and, as he grew up, was his father's right hand around their small holding, helping him to plant and reap the crops they grew for their sustenance, and helping him with the animals he reared for their livelihood. Though he helped with everything, his real interest and love were the pigs. He spent much time looking after them, even sometimes to the absolute neglect of the goats and the cows. He had managed to learn to read and write well, learnt arithmetic and times tables, but not much else and it was soon obvious that he would have to depend on farming for his future support.

All went well with the family, until when Jacob was in his mid-twenties, his father died suddenly of a heart attack one Easter Monday. It happened at a cricket match he attended a few miles away. In the height of the excitement when the team he was backing was winning the match, he was enjoying himself watching his star batsmen piling up a big score. He and Teacher, Manager, JP Howell, Parson and all his friends sheltered under the big breadfruit tree on the little rise at the edge of the cricket ground. He was cheering and clapping and calling out his encouragement when he slumped from the chair he was sitting on. Before they could get him to the doctor five miles away, he was gone to glory.

You can imagine what a difficult time it was for Miss Clarry, and moreso for Jacob. He had lost his father and more than all, his very best friend. Miss Conse, seeing them coming up from the graveside, said, "Ahi Miss Clarry a feel it fi yu and you to Jacob. You have to be the man now an teck over from you father, and teck care of yu modder."

It was as if that was what Jacob needed, the death of his father, or the words from Miss Conse, or both. He took on a new lease on life, stepping into his fathers place, to everyone's surprise and some amount of delight. His love for animals, especially his pigs, became his life. He soon started to breed and rear pigs in earnest. He sold out the few cows and the twenty goats and with that money he established a proper pig farm. His devotion to his pigs and his skill at rearing them soon earned him the reputation as a successful pig farmer. He even won prizes given by the agricultural society. His father had discovered from early, when Jacob was a small boy, his love for animals, particularly pigs, and taught him well.

Even though he learned about the cows and the goats, it was clear his favourite was pigs, maybe because they were penned up in a sty, so he didn't have to go looking for them in the pasture, especially on a rainy day, or to make sure that in the mornings they were turned out to feed and in the evenings to bring them to the pen for the night. Pigs were different – they remained in the sty where he could always see them and tend them. And the way he kept his pigpen was an example to all. People talked about it near and far. Teacher Foster brought the boys from his animal husbandry class to see this model pigpen, which Jacob had constructed himself, and the Agricultural Officer brought many persons who were thinking of going into pig rearing to see it.

Inside this forty foot square pen was a sheltered concrete area sloping down to a dirt area where water could settle and provide a good mud bath for the pigs. The concrete area was divided into several stalls for the boar, sows and their newborn. The feeding and watering troughs were set along one side so Jacob could feed the pigs and clean the troughs without going into the pen. A smaller pen, about twenty feet from this one, was built on similar lines. A third pen housed the ones being prepared for the butcher. Each had a small shade tree which he had planted nearby.

No one knew from where he got all these ideas. As Miss Conse remarked, "It look like im a get some guidance." Ever so often, as he thought necessary, he would take his bucket and broom and scrub out the sties so they were always clean. The pig's dung he collected and made a compost heap for his vegetables, and when the water in the dirt area became too much he opened small channels to drain it off into the field. Truly a model, and as Miss Conse observed, "Den if im can do all dat im not so fool after all, wha no ded no call it duppy."

Jacob's reputation as a model pig farmer amazed everyone, and that fame spread far and wide. His pigs were healthy and thriving and butchers came from near and far seeking his pigs. Sometimes when the pigs were ready and they didn't come he had them slaughtered, gave away some pork and the fifth quarter, sold some and made corned pork which again was well received by his customers. Because he reared the pigs himself he could afford to sell below the shop price. He would do regular checks to see what they were selling for and price his meat below. He made a special fireplace and smoked some of the corned pork with pimento leaves, and this he sold at a higher price than the regular one.

No doubt about it, Jacob had come into his own earning a good living for himself and his ageing mother whom he took really good care of. And this, by doing something he liked to do. "The only thing Jacob love better dan him pig dem is im modder." That was Miss Conse holding forth as usual.

But as was the custom or tradition in the district, as it was in every district in the island, his activity earned him a nickname. And the names they gave Jacob were many – "Pork man, Pig man, Corn Pork man, Corn pork ruler, Corn pork king, Corn Pork Jesas". This latter one met the disapproval of many, including Miss Conse. "Dat nat right, leave mi Jesas outa dis." Finally the district settled on "Corn Pork Doctor", and that was what he was called by everyone.

Strangely, Jacob himself did not eat pork. He ate every kind of meat except pork. Some thought he was "Rasta" or "Seven day". He made an exception for gungo soup which he loved. He would eat the soup made with the pork, but he would not eat a morsel of the meat. He once confessed that it was the love for his pigs that kept him from eating pork. It was bad enough, he said, to have to butcher them, but he could not bring himself to eat their flesh. His love for his pigs was legendary, as was his devotion and care for his mother, now bedridden. "Is hard to say it, but is the best thing ever happen to him when im puppa ded, it meck im into a real summady, a real man," Miss Conse said.

Time went on and his mother died. He was devastated. But after he buried her in style in the churchyard beside his father, it was amazing to see how quickly he seemed to come back to himself, and it was business as usual. As he had no other relative in the district, his uncle, his mother's youngest brother, after about a year, took him to live with him in Kingston. His wife had died childless about a year before his sister, Jacob's mother, and he was living alone in a comfortable and spacious house in a decent part of the city. He had loved Jacob as his own child and regarded him as such ever since he was born. They got along splendidly together and his uncle often said to his friends how lucky he was to have Jacob to share his house and life.

Jacob had sold the pigs, leaving just a few with his lifelong friend whom he left in charge of the property when he went to live with his uncle. Jacob soon came out of his accustomed shyness, started going to church with his uncle, made many friends at church and around. He was happy, but he missed the country life. He missed his pigs most of all, and he was sad because he had to depend on his uncle for everything. Pig rearing was the only way he knew to make a living and thought he would like to do that, rear a few in the spacious backyard. But his uncle told him that it was against the law to rear pigs in the town area. Then his uncle suggested, "Why you don't sell corn pork? We could buy the meat in Coronation market or Cross Roads and sell corn pork."

At first Jacob said no, but the more he thought about it, the more he liked the idea. His uncle suggested that they could keep the corn pork barrel in the garage which was empty anyway. So Jacob got a wooden barrel, made a cover and, along with a makeshift table of plywood he set up in the garage with his scale and chopping block, he was ready for business.

At first the sales were slow, but it was not long before word spread and his corn pork became famous on his road, in the next street and all around and soon he was doing a brisk and thriving business. But Jacob thought he could do even better and he bought another scale, another barrel, corned more pork and, rather than wait for the customers to come, he would walk to other streets in his area and in nearby Vineyard Town. He bought a plastic pail with a lid in which he carried the meat. He did this for only half a day on Thursdays and Saturdays but it proved so rewarding that he soon bought a bicycle fitted with a special carrier, and extended his territory to include Woodford Park, Allman Town and Kingston Gardens. As he went from street to street, the voice of Corn Pork Doctor could be heard singing a ditty he made up to announce his presence. "Whey money gone, whey money gone, corn pork a pass gungo soup remedy, gungo soup remedy."

People loved to hear him. Many bought his pork because of the song. Children on some streets sang with him, and he loved them for it. For years, this familiar sound heralded the desired product and, as the saying goes, he did not have hands to sell it. Sometimes he even went as far as Swallowfield and Cross Roads. Business was so good, he made arrangements for the meat to be delivered to his house. At special times like August and Christmas, he made the train journey to his native village to purchase, by arrangement, whole carcasses of pork from persons whom, over the years, he had assisted to start their own pig rearing, including his friend whom he had left in charge of his property and who, by all accounts, was doing quite well with his pig rearing. As his present business grew he had them rear pigs specially to supply his needs.

His uncle was so pleased that he suggested that they put up a little shop on the premises since the area was becoming commercialized and he was now outgrowing the space in the garage. Jacob agreed, but wanted to make the shop bigger than his uncle's plan since he would like to expand and sell other types of meat, fresh and pickled. And so the shop was built, and the Big City Meat shop was established. The business prospered and in a few years it had outgrown the shop.

His uncle, now frail and aged, got ill and Jacob took really good care of him. "Just like how im do fi im modder.

Gawd mus bless im," Miss Conse said as she got the news. For that and for his fairness in conducting his business, his pleasant manner, Jacob was well respected by all who knew him, people in his church and in the surroundings.

One day, a gentleman in a gray suit appeared at the shop and asked for his uncle. When Jacob enquired who he was, he said he was his uncle's friend. Leaving his assistant in the shop, Jacob escorted him into his uncle's room. "Uncle C, one of yu friends come look for yu."

"Who dat? Oh, is you Mista Cox, come in...Jacob give im a seat, and you siddung here too, dis concern yu."

They both sat down and as Mr. Cox accepted the chair he offered, he said to Jacob, "Actually, I am your uncle's lawyer, I've been his lawyer for over twenty-five years." He sat down and opened his brief case took out a document and continued. "Well, Mr. Thomas, everything is here as you said. The property here will go to Jacob your nephew, along with the money in the bank, and the house in Barbican is to be sold and the money used to bury you and pay your lawful debt."

Jacob could not believe what he was hearing. "Uncle C, you mean you give me everything?"

"Yu deserve it mi son. You is all the relative I have. And I couldn't want a better son dan you, but there is a stipulation. Show im di plan Mr. Cox."

Mr. Cox unfolded a blue print. "Dat is di plan for the building yu going to build on the open lot dat you will also get on Queen Street. Is a better business spot dan here. You wi live upstairs an have the business downstairs just like Mr. Wang down Pole Street. Yu will have enough money to build the building, wid a cold room at the back for storing the meat, and when yu sell dis you will have money to buy equipment, refrigerators, deep freeze an di like and pay off for di new building. Mr. Cox and im people will help yu. There is one final thing when di building done," and he completed his instructions.

Soon after that, the old man died, and everything was done according to his wishes. When the building was completed, Mr. Cox arranged for the sign painter to do the final thing as instructed. On the front of the building, in bold letters was painted "Uncle Cee's Big City Meat Store".

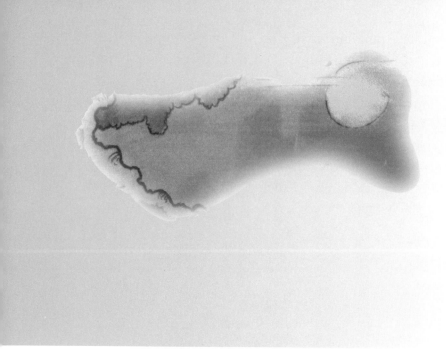

Solo Dance

Down on the common
On the grass soft and green
Easter Monday like always
Was picnic day
Every year same scene
From long as memory
Nice things, nice time, nice food
Snowball and Frisco
Fry fritters and toto
Gingerbeer and aerated water
Plenty people, plenty music, plenty dancing
Merriment and fun
Under the big spreading guango tree.

Maypole set up, string up
Young and old alike
Jollificate enjoy themselves dancing away
Clear clear day no rain
Not even a cloud
Fun and laughter ringing
Bamboo fife rhumba box
Shack shack drum and singing
Raising cain
It was well into evening-brown dusk
When the sounds of laughter and the music ceased
The maypole ribbons left flirting in the gentle breeze.

But the sad young girl on the hill
Could only look down on the fun
Could only listen all day long
To the sweet music
Floating up the hillside loud and clear
Wiping a tear now and then
Remembering those times when
Her mother now dead
Lead her and the others in the dance on picnic day.
How she loved to dance
But they took her away
For she was mental
Her wicked husband told them so
Jealous of her village fame
And the smiles she gave to all.

He was a hard, cruel man
Who said his daughter was also strange
Like her mother off her head
So he chained her he said

235

To the tree in the yard
So she wouldn't hurt herself
So she couldn't go dancing that day.

Early Tuesday morning
As the sun was coming up
People passing the common
Saw the young girl in her sleeping clothes
Alone
Dancing the Maypole
To the compelling memory
Of yesterday's music
Patterning her mother's dance, step for step
Move for move, stance for stance
Losing not a movement nor a beat
To the amusement and delight
And the marvel of all who saw.

All day she danced
In the sun's full heat
Without pausing, without stopping
This was her moment
He face told the story
As did her body
Her Spirit floated in the dance
So like her mother she moved
With ease and grace
Plaiting and unplaiting
The bright ribbons one by one
Each over the other
Over and over again and again
Not hearing those who called
Not seeing those who waved.

Her solo dance continued unabated
Till exhausted she fell
To the soft green grass
And laid still as if in sleep

The red Maypole ribbon
Well clutched in her stiff fingers still
The others in concert with the breeze
Gently caressing her cold cold face
Etched with contentment joy and ecstacy
Her unforgiving father
Fetched to the spot
Felt her cold feet
Roughly brushed a ribbon
From her smiling mouth
Saw her pearl-white teeth
And the tiny black ants
Making her one with the earth.